Amnesty

Amnesty

EDITED BY

Dee Mitchell

Published 1993 by Minerva Australia
a part of Reed Books Australia
22 Salmon Street, Port Melbourne, Victoria 3207
a division of Reed International Books Australia Pty Limited

Reprinted 1994

Typeset in Perpetua by Bookset Pty Ltd
Printed and bound in Australia by Australian Print Group

National Library of Australia
cataloguing-in-publication data:

Amnesty: an original and powerful collection of new writing.
ISBN 1 86330 287 5.

1. Short stories, Australia. I. Mitchell, Dee, 1943– .
A 823.010803

Acknowledgements

Thea Astley 'Heart is Where the Home Is', from *It's Raining in Mango* published by Penguin Books Australia, 1989.

Sara Dowse 'Dough' forthcoming from *Safar: To Count*, to be published by Penguin Books Australia, 1994.

Suzanne Edgar 'A Proposed Marriage', from *Counting Backwards*, published by University of Queensland Press, 1991.

Tom Keneally 'The Man Who Knew Walesa' in *Prize Writing (An Original Collection of Writings by Past Winners to Celebrate 21 Years of the Booker Prize)*, edited and introduced by Martyn Goff, published by Hodder & Stoughton, London 1989.

Morris West from *The Shoes of the Fisherman*, published by William Heinemann, 1963.

Contents

Preface

As you read this men, women and children throughout the world live in terror of a doorknock in the middle of the night. They live in fear of being thrown into prison without charge or trial; of torture, death or of their loved ones 'disappearing' after being taken into custody.

It is easy to feel helpless and to ask what difference can I make to the plight of the persecuted, to those victims of terror and the often forgotten prisoners of conscience. To paraphrase a Chinese saying, every journey no matter how long begins with a single step. It is therefore vital for each of us to take that first step along with more than 1,100,000 other individuals in over 150 countries, who support Amnesty International and who work together to prevent the violations by governments of their citizens' fundamental human rights.

Amnesty International provides many ways for every individual to act — locally, nationally and internationally. This is the fulcrum around which its ability turns to create change, to quietly but persistently challenge offending governments, and above all to influence them to respect their citizens' basic rights, irrespective of race, nation, political persuasion or religious beliefs.

One of Amnesty International's strengths is the preservation of total impartiality. To maintain this it does not accept funding from any government source but relies on donations from individuals and its membership. This collection of writings is just one more way of drawing attention to those who need our help. It is not intended to be a tome of gloom and doom, but a consciousness- and fund-raising venture. Amnesty International is indebted to the authors for their spontaneous and generous contributions to this, another chapter in the continuing conspiracy of hope.

Dee Mitchell

Canberra 1993

May Amnesty never fade into oblivion

MANNING CLARK

The *Oxford English Dictionary* defines amnesty as a general pardon, especially for a political offence.

In a perfect world, people who disagreed with each other on political, religious or even artistic questions would not torture, imprison or cause any irreparable harm to their opponents. In a perfect world, men and women would accept the Greek ideal — that is, they would not put on black looks towards their neighbour when he or she behaves in any way that offends them.

But the world in which we live is far from perfect. Those who believe they know the truth are often driven to practise abominations against those who disagree with them. Communists put dissidents into labour camps where, if they do not mend their ways, they will stay until the day they die. Some communities imprison or even remove the heads of transgressors against their Ten Commandments. Conservative governments in some parts of the world jail and torture their critics.

The great virtue of Amnesty International is that they do try to rescue the victims of political and religious persecution from their tormentors. Thanks to their efforts, men and women have been rescued from terrifying ordeals in the jails and interrogation chambers where the servants of the powerful carry out their monstrous work.

So Amnesty International deserves our support. That means money and that means not turning a blind eye or a deaf ear to what is going on in the world.

It is perhaps significant that the English word amnesty derives from the Greek word *amnestia*, which means oblivion. Oblivion on our part is probably just as great a sin as that committed by the bully boys and girls in the torture chambers of the world.

We need here an Amnesty Australia to redeem the cruelty by some policemen towards Aborigines, as well as by those who cannot tolerate any lifestyle different from their own. We are in no position to thank our gods that we are not as other people. Imprisonment for political or religious opinions and the torture of such victims concerns the whole human race.

Amnesty International has worked long and well to help those victims. We must also work to remove the causes that drive human beings to commit such bestialities against each other. Perhaps we should start at home.

Heart is Where the Home Is

THEA ASTLEY

The morning the men came, policemen, someone from the government, to take the children away from the black camp up along the river, first there was the wordless terror of heart-jump, then the wailing, the women scattering and trying to run dragging their kids, the men sullen, powerless before this new white law they'd never heard of. Even the coppers felt lousy seeing all those yowling gins. They'd have liked the boongs to show a bit of fight, really, then they could have laid about feeling justified.

But no. The buggers just took it. Took it and took it.

The passivity finally stuck in their guts.

Bidgi Mumbler's daughter-in-law grabbed her little boy and fled through the scrub patch towards the river.

Her skinny legs didn't seem to move fast enough across that world of the policeman's eye. She knew what was going to happen. It had happened just the week before at a camp near Tobaccotown. Her cousin Ruthie lost a kid that way.

'We'll bring her up real good,' they'd told Ruthie. 'Take her away to big school and teach her proper, eh? You like your kid to grow up proper and know about Jesus?'

Ruthie had been slammed into speechlessness.

Who were they?

She didn't understand. She knew only this was her little girl. There was all them words, too many of them, and then the hands.

There had been a fearful tug-o'-war: the mother clinging to the little girl, the little girl clutching her mother's dress, and the welfare officer with the police, all pulling, the kid howling, the other mothers egg-eyed, gripping their own kids, petrified, no men around, the men tricked out of camp.

Ruthie could only whimper, but then, as the policeman started to drag her child away to the buggy, she began a screeching that opened up the sky and pulled it down on her.

She bin chase that buggy two miles till one of the police he ride back on his horse an shout at her an when she wouldn take no notice she bin run run run an he gallop after her an hit her one two, cracka cracka, with his big whip right across the face so the pain get all muddle with the cryin and she run into the trees beside the track where he couldn follow. She kep goin after that buggy, fightin her way through scrub but it wasn't no good. They too fast. An then the train it come down the line from Tobaccotown an that was the last she see her little girl, two black legs an arms, strugglin as the big white man he lift her into carriage from the sidin.

'You'll have other baby,' Nelly Mumbler comforted her. 'You'll have other baby.' But Ruthie kept sittin, wouldn do nothin. Jus sit an rock an cry an none of the other women they couldn help, their kids gone too and the men so angry they jus drank when they could get it an their rage burn like scrub fire.

Everything gone. Land. Hunting grounds. River. Fish. Gone. New god come. Old talk still about killings. The old ones remembering the killings.

'Now they take our kids,' Jackie Mumbler said to his father, Bidgi. 'We make kids for whites now. Can't they make their own kids, eh? Take everythin. Land. Kids. Don't give nothin, only take.'

So Nelly had known the minute she saw them whites comin down the track. The other women got scared, fixed to the spot like they grow there, all shakin and whimperin. Stuck. 'You'll be trouble,' they warned. 'You'll be trouble.'

'Don't care,' she said. 'They not takin my kid.'

She wormed her way into the thickest part of the rain forest, following the river, well away from the track up near the packers' road. Her baby held tightly against her chest, she stumbled through vine and over root, slashed by leaves and thorns, her eyes wide with fright, the baby crying in little gulps, nuzzling in at her straining body.

There'd bin other time year before she still hear talk about. All them livin up near Tinwon. The govmin said for them all to come long train. Big surprise, eh, an they all gone thinkin tobacco, tucker, blankets. An the men, they got all the men out early that day help work haulin trees up that loggin camp and the women they all excited waitin long that train, all the kids playin, and then them two policemen they come an start grabbin, grabbin all the kids, every kid, and the kids they screamin an the women they all cryin an tuggin an some, they hittin themselves with little sticks. One of the police, he got real angry and start shovin the women back hard. He push an push an then the train pulls out while they pushin an they can see the kids clutchin at the windows and some big white woman inside that train, she pull them back.

Nelly dodged through wait-a-while, stinging-bush, still hearing the yells of the women back at the camp. Panting and gasping, she came down to the water where a sand strip ran half way across the river. If she crossed she would only leave tracks. There was no time to scrape away telltale footprints. She crept back into the rain forest and stood trembling, squeezing her baby tightly, trying to smother his howls, but the baby wouldn't hush, so she huddled under a bush and comforted him with her nipples for a while, his round eyes staring up at her as he sucked while she regained her breath.

Shouts wound through the forest like vines.

Wailing filtered through the canopy.

Suddenly a dog yelped, too close. She pulled herself to her feet, the baby still sucking, and went staggering along the sandy track by the riverbank, pushing her bony body hard, thrusting between claws of branch and thorn, a half mile, a mile, until she knew that soon the forest cover would finish and she'd be out on the fence-line of George Laffey's place, the farm old Bidgi Mumbler had come up and worked for. She'd been there too, now and then, help washin, cleanin, when young Missus Laffey makin all them pickles an things.

For a moment she stood uncertain by the fence, then on impulse she thrust her baby under the wire and wriggled through after him, smelling the grass, smelling ants, dirt, all those living things, and then she grabbed him up and stumbled through the cow paddock down to the mango trees, down past the hen yard, the vegetable garden, down over a lawn with flower-blaze and the felty shadows of tulip trees, past Mister Laffey spading away, not stopping when he looked up at her, startled, but gasping past him round the side of the house to the back steps and the door that was always open.

Mag Laffey came to the doorway and the two young women watched each other in a racket of insect noise. A baby was crying in a back room and a small girl kept tugging at her mother's skirts.

The missus was talkin, soft and fast. Nelly couldn't hear nothin and then hands, they pull her in, gently, gently, but she too frightened hangin onto Charley, not lettin go till the white missus she put them hands on her shoulders and press her down onto one them kitchen chairs an hold her. 'Still, now,' her voice keep sayin. 'Still.'

So she keep real still and the pretty white missus say, 'Tell me, Nelly. You tell me what's the matter.'

It took a while, the telling, between the snuffles and the coaxing and the gulps and swallowed horrors.

'I see,' Mag Laffey said at last. 'I see,' she said again, her lips tightening. 'Oh I see.'

She eased the baby from Nelly's arms and put him down on the floor with her own little girl, watching with a smile as the children stared then reached out to touch each other. She went over to the stove and filled the teapot and handed the black girl a cup, saying, 'You drink that right up now and then we'll think of something. George will think of something.'

———•———

It was half an hour before the policemen came.

They rode down the track from the railway line at an aggressive trot, coming to halt beside George as he rested on his spade.

Confronted with their questions he went blank. 'Only the housegirl.' And added, 'And Mag and the kids.'

The police kicked their horses on through his words and George slammed his spade hard into the turned soil and followed them down to where they were tethering their horses at the stair rails. He could see them boot-thumping up the steps. The house lay open as a palm.

Mag forestalled them, coming out onto the verandah. Her whole body was a challenge.

'Well,' she asked, 'what is it?'

The big men fidgeted. They'd had brushes with George Laffey's wife before, so deceptively young and pliable, a woman who never knew her place, always airing an idea of some sort. Not knowing George's delight with her, they felt sorry for that poor bastard of a husband who'd come rollicking home a few years back from a trip down south with a town girl with town notions.

'Government orders, missus,' one said. 'We have to pick up all the abo kids. All abo kids have got to be taken to special training schools. It's orders.'

Mag Laffey inspected their over-earnest faces. She couldn't help smiling.

'Are you asking me, sergeant, if I have any half-caste children, or do I misunderstand?' She could hardly wait for their reaction.

The sergeant bit his lower lip and appeared to chew something before he could answer. 'Not you personally, missus.' *Disgusting*, he thought, *disgusting piece of goods, making suggestions like that*. 'We just want to know if you have any round the place? Any belonging to that lot up at the camp?'

'Why would I do that?'

'I don't know, missus.' He went stolid. 'You've got a housegirl, haven't you? Your husband said.'

'Yes, I do.'

'Well then, has she got any kids?'

'Not that I'm aware of,' Mag Laffey lied vigorously. Her eyes met theirs with amused candour.

'Maybe so. But we'd like to speak to her. You know it's breaking the law to conceal this.'

'Certainly I know.' George was standing behind the men at the foot of the steps, his face nodding her on. 'You're wasting your time here, let me tell you. You're wasting mine as well. But that's what government's for, isn't it?'

'I don't know what you mean, missus.' His persistence moved him forward a step. 'Can we see that girl or not?'

Mag called over her shoulder down the hall but stood her ground at the doorway, listening to Nelly shuffle, unwilling, along the lino. When she came up to the men, she still had a dishcloth in her hands that dripped suds onto the floor. Her eyes would not meet those of the big men blocking the light.

'Where's your kid, Mary?' the sergeant asked, bullying and jocular. 'You hiding your kid?'

Nelly dropped her head and shook it dumbly.

'Cat got your tongue?' the other man said. 'You not wantem talk, eh? You lying?'

'She has no children,' Mag Laffey interrupted coldly. 'I told you that. Perhaps the cat has your ears as well. If you shout and nag and humiliate her, you'll never get an answer. Can't you understand something as basic as that? You're frightening her.'

She looked past the two of them at her husband who was smiling his support.

'Listen, lady,' the sergeant said, his face congested with the suppressed need to punch this cheeky sheila right down her own hallway, 'that's not what they tell me at the camp.'

'What's not what they tell you?'

'She's got a kid all right. She's hiding it some place.'

George's eyes, she saw, were strained with affection and concern. *Come up*, her own eyes begged him. *Come up*. 'Sergeant,' she said, 'I have known Nelly since she was a young girl. She's helped out here for the last four years. Do you think I wouldn't know if she had a child? Do you? But you're free to search the house, if you want, and the grounds. You're thirsting for it, aren't you, warrant or not?'

The men shoved roughly past her at that, flattening Nelly Mumbler against the wall, and creaked down the hallway, into bedrooms and parlour and out into the kitchen. Cupboard doors crashed open. There was a banging of washhouse door.

George came up the steps and took his wife's arm, steering her and Nelly to the back of the house and putting them behind him as he watched the police come in from the yard.

'Satisfied?'

'No, we're not, mate,' the sergeant replied nastily. 'Not one bloody bit.'

Their powerful bodies crowded the kitchen out. They watched contemptuously as Nelly crept back to the sink, her body tensed with fright.

'We don't believe you, missus,' the sergeant said. 'Not you or your hubby. There'll be real trouble for both of you when we catch you out.'

Mag held herself braced against infant squawls that might expose them at any minute. She made herself busy stoking the stove.

'Righto,' George said, pressing her arm and looking sharp and hard at the other men. 'You've had your look. Now would you mind leaving. We've all got work to get on with.'

The sergeant was sulky. He scraped his boots about and kept glancing around the kitchen and out the door into the back garden. The Laffeys' small girl was getting under his feet and pulling at his trouser legs, driving him crazy.

'All right,' he agreed reluctantly. 'All right.' He gave one last stare at Nelly's back. 'Fuckin' boongs,' he said, deliberately trying to offend that stuck-up Mrs Laffey. 'More trouble than they're worth. And that's bloody nothing.'

The two women remained rooted in the kitchen while George went back up the track to his spadework. The sound of the horses died away.

At the sink Nelly kept washing and washing, her eyes never leaving the suds, the dishmop, the plate she endlessly scoured. Even after the thud of hoof faded beyond the ridge, even after that. And even after Mag Laffey took a cloth and began wiping the dishes and stacking them in the cupboard, even after that.

Mag saw her husband come round the side of the

house, toss his hat on an outside peg and sit on the top step to ease his earth-stuck clobbers of boots off. Nelly's stiffly curved back asked question upon question. Her long brown fingers asked. Her turned-away face asked. When her baby toddled back into the kitchen, taken down from the bedroom ceiling manhole where George had hidden him with a lolly to suck, Nelly stayed glued to that sink washing that one plate.

'Come on, Nelly,' Mag said softly. 'What's the matter? We've beaten them, haven't we?'

George had picked up the small black boy and his daughter and was bouncing a child on each knee, waggling his head lovingly between them both while small hands pawed his face.

Infinitely slowly, Nelly turned from the sink, her fingers dripping soap and water. She looked at George Laffey cuddling a white baby and a black but she couldn't smile. 'Come nex time,' she said, hopeless. 'Come nex time.'

George and his wife looked at her with terrible pity. They knew this as well. They knew.

'And we'll do the same next time,' Mag Laffey stated. 'You don't have to worry.'

Then George Laffey said, 'You come live here, Nelly. You come all time, eh?' His wife nodded at each word. Nodded and smiled and cried a bit. 'You and Charley, eh?'

Nelly opened her mouth and wailed. *What is it?* they kept asking. *What's the matter? Wouldn't you like that?* They told her she could have the old store shed down by the river. They'd put a stove in and make it proper. Nelly kept crying, her dark eyes an unending fountain, and at last George became exasperated.

'You've got no choice, Nelly,' he said, dropping the

baby pidgin he had never liked anyway. 'You've got no choice. If you come here we can keep an eye on Charley. If you don't, the government men will take him away. You don't want that, do you? Why don't you want to come?'

'Don't want to leave my family,' she sobbed. 'Don't want.'

'God love us,' George cried from the depths of his nonunderstanding, 'God love us, they're only a mile up the river.' He could feel his wife's fingers warning on his arm. 'You can see them whenever you want.'

'It's not the same,' Nelly insisted and sobbed. 'Not same.'

George thought he understood. He said, 'You want Jackie, then. You want your husband to come along too, work in the garden maybe? Is that it?'

He put the baby into her arms and the two of them rocked sombrely before him. He still hadn't understood.

The old men old women uncles aunts cousins brothers sisters tin humpies bottles dogs dirty blankets tobacco handouts fights river trees all the tribe's remnants and wretchedness, destruction and misery.

Her second skin now.

'Not same,' she whispered. And she cried them centuries of tribal dreams in those two words. 'Not same.'

The Monkey Man

—◆—

BRYCE COURTENAY

At the tag end of the Great Depression, the three of us, my mother, sister Rosemary-Ann and I, lived in a single room with a make-shift kitchenette without running water, behind a kaffir shop owned by a Jew we respectfully called, Mr Polanski.

Everybody called Mr Polanski's shop 'The Jew Shop', which my ma said was not a nice thing to say about a precious man like Mr Polanski. The shop was in a small town in the Northern Transvaal, a part of South Africa which is usually dismissed by people who come from other places with a sniff and a superior grin.

I remember how the kindly little Jew would speak English to us, but always in a low voice, darting a furtive look over his shoulder after each sentence, as though afraid of being overheard in this place where English was a forbidden language and where only the *taal* was spoken, the guttural, harsh Afrikaans of the backveldt Boers.

My mother was suffering from a severe bout of malaria and lay in a state of delirium in the small, dark room. Rosemary-Ann, my six-and-a-half-year-old sister, was nursing her, covering her body with a wet sheet every hour or so to cool down the malarial furnace that raged under her skin.

We'd soak the sheet in a large white enamel basin in the backyard which I'd filled with an empty jam tin from a tap set against the back wall of Mr Polanski's shop. We'd dunk the sheet into the basin, punching all the white air pockets back under the water until it was thoroughly soaked. Then I'd take one side and Rosemary-Ann the other and we'd wring the sheet out, holding on tight as anything and twisting until our wrists ached and our fingers lost all their strength and we couldn't stand it a moment longer. Then we'd carry the sheet, twisted like a liquorice stick, inside to where my mother lay. There we'd untwist it and wrap it around her naked, shivering body. In an hour it would be dry again — how she could be hot enough to dry out a sheet in an hour and still shiver with her teeth chattering like billyo was a mystery to me. But that's malaria for you.

Whenever my ma came to, I'd lift her head and Rosemary-Ann would bring a mug of water to her cracked lips. The mug would set up a sort of timpani as her teeth chinged and chinted twenty to the dozen on it's enamel rim, causing the water to spill over her trembling lip and splash down into the space between her small, flat breasts. Not that this mattered, because she was soaking already from sweat, with her hair stuck to her forehead and wet at the nape of her neck.

Once Rosemary-Ann tried to get her to take a quinine tablet which stuck on her dry tongue and stayed there even when we tried to splash it down her throat with a mug of water.

From early morning the heat beat down from the corrugated iron roof and the room became very hot, bottle flies, blue and bloated, buzzed in and out of the door every time we went into the backyard. When I wasn't filling the basin or helping to wring out the sheet I was swatting flies with a yellow flyswatter, creeping up on them and . . . *Blat!*

Quite how we came to be in the small room with my mother dying of malaria I was too young at the time to understand. And again, just how long we had been living like this, on Marie biscuits and Klim, a brand of pow-dered milk, I also can't say. Children have no sense of time, perhaps for four or five days over a holiday period. It seems unlikely that it could have been much longer or we would have been discovered by Mr Polanski or his dog.

Mr Polanski had a fox terrier named Billy who once sat for a whole weekend alone in the shop with his nose resting on a Marmite cracker because Mr Polanski, who had trained him only to eat something after a password was said, hadn't said the password. What I mean is, Billy would come around and visit us even though we couldn't give him things to eat, because we didn't know the password, but this time we hadn't seen him for ages and so Mr Polanski may have been away or something.

I recall only that it was morning when the giant came, just after I'd returned from having a piss in the backyard, where, by the way, I'd traced a perfect figure eight in the plopping red dust at my feet without getting even a drop on my toes. There was a sudden and loud knock on the corrugated iron door of the tiny make-shift kitchenette.

I opened the door to look directly into the moleskin kneecaps of what appeared to be a giant.

The knees stepped back two paces as the door opened fully and I was able to look heavenwards where I observed the giant looking down at me with piercing blue eyes and a waterfall of white hair which cascaded in waves almost to his waist and which was as white as a Father Christmas beard.

I'd heard some talk about Christmas around the place, but my mother had become increasingly ill so the talk had stopped and Christmas just seemed to have gone away. The giant straddling the doorway wore no pixie cap puddled on his head. Even allowing that he would have been mad to wear his fur-trimmed coat in the heat, his hands hung free so he quite obviously wasn't carrying a bag of toys over his shoulder.

This, I quickly decided, was no Father Christmas, that was for sure. Around the giant's pink mouth his beard was stained yellow from chewing tobacco. His huge hands ended well above my head and his arms, burned black in the sun, were coated with a dense matting of dark hair and stretched back from his wrists as thick and muscled as Popeye's, or even more so, like those of the terrible, black-stubbled Bluto.

The giant placed one of his huge hands on my head and looking up I could see through the gaps in his fingers. It was as though I was standing beside the trunk of a huge tree observing the sun's sharp rays through thick, dark branches that smelled of nicotine and engine oil.

My five-year-old imagination knew just enough to sense that we were in a lot of trouble, for I was beginning to suspect that far from being Father Christmas, this was the giant in *Jack and the Beanstalk*.

Fee-fi-fo-fum, I smell the blood of an Englishman.
Be he alive or be he dead, I'll grind his bones to make my
bread.

He removed his hand from my head and spoke in Afrikaans, which was the first time I'd realised that the giant in *Jack and the Beanstalk* was an Afrikaner, though I must say, when you thought about it, this was pretty obvious.

Rosemary-Ann had come to stand behind me and as neither of us spoke Afrikaans we looked at him blankly. Then Rosemary-Ann asked him, using one of the few Afrikaans words she knew, 'Can you speak English, please, *Meneer*?'

He paused and pulled his thick pink lips into a straight disapproving line, elongating the yellow tobacco stain around his mouth. Then he cleared his throat, a sound like small boulders rattling in a concrete mixer and his words, when they came, seemed an effort, as though he was trying to hold down something he found quite abhorrent, like boiled cabbage.

'Sick? You mama, she sick, ja?'

'Oh, yes, she is going to die,' I said, unaware of the meaning of death but knowing that it was something that happened to people who became very sick, probably with malaria.

Rosemary-Ann nodded, not knowing what to make of the giant who now stepped right up to the door again so that his head and the top of his shoulders were well above the lintel.

An enormous headless presence filled the space around us and gave off the pungent odour of sweat and a second, sweeter smell, of tobacco cured in molasses. His moleskins were strapped by a wide leather belt, fixed with a large square buckle at the centre. Though this was not where his trousers ended, they continued for another six inches beyond the sweat-oiled belt and big brass buckle, splaying outwards and turning themselves inside out to show a stained, dirty cotton lining. Arranged on either side of his fly were two large braces buttons of mottled grey bone. The giant's great tummy sat like an egg within this comfortable looking nest of soft, turned inside out, moleskin.

Suddenly his hairy calloused hands, with crackled, black-rimmed nails, moved downwards towards us, but stopped just short and grasped his trousers above his knees. The giant's legs began to buckle until his shoulders and beard appeared from above the lintel and almost immediately a great red face topped with a shining bald head followed. Close up like this, with his huge frame filling the door space, I was able to identify him immediately, I'm telling you for sure, there was simply no mistaking him, this was the giant out of *Jack and the Beanstalk*, I was one hundred per cent certain.

The giant, now almost on his haunches, moved forward, a hand as big as a road worker's shovel, pushing us gently aside. Twisting his shoulders, he forced his body through the small doorway into the darkened kitchen space beyond. Once inside, he rose again, his great bald head bumping the tin roof and making a sharp discordant metallic sound that made the whole room jump. He stooped and rubbed his head briefly before moving to where my mother lay shaking and raffling.

I was later to learn that Oupa Winterbach was seven foot and a bit inches tall and weighed three hundred and twenty-five pounds. He stood for a moment looking down at my unconscious mother, running his hand pensively through his beard so that the silver hair seemed to grow like magic out of the top of his fist. Then he pronounced the single word, 'malaria'.

He waited, as though expecting some sort of response from my mother, perhaps a confirmation? But when none came he cleared his throat and introduced himself. 'Winterbach, missus!' Then he added, 'Cornelius Winterbach,' as though the appending of his Christian name somehow legitimised this introduction to the groaning, delirious woman who lay on the packing case bed at his feet, her fever-bright eyes staring vacantly up at him.

The giant stood for a moment longer then, as though he'd come to a sudden decision, he wiped the back of his hand across his mouth and bending, scooped my ma from the bed, the wet sheet clinging to her naked body. In his great hairy, sunburned Bluto arms, she seemed to be no larger than a small child.

'You can't eat her, she isn't dead yet,' I said, starting to blub.

'Kom kinder!' he commanded in a huge, gruff voice, forcing us ahead of him with a jerk of his beard. We had few clothes anyway, but we left without them. Perhaps they were fetched later, I don't recall. All I knew was that we'd been captured by a terrible giant and they're not the sort of people who wait around while you pack a suitcase.

I gripped Rosemary-Ann's hand tightly and we followed him outside to where a Model-T Ford stood parked in the street. The ancient vehicle had been converted into a flat-bed truck and a large African woman sat in the back. Seeing us approach she stood up to reveal a narrow mattress which occupied about half the width of the truck.

The sight of the black woman cheered me up immediately. As a small child I'd had a Zulu wet nurse and nanny and I knew from first-hand experience that people with large black breasts and smiling white teeth looked after little boys and didn't ever harm them, not even beat them when they were bad.

The giant said something to her in Shangaani and she smiled shyly and removed from around her waist a square of blue cotton ticking which she appeared to be wearing as an extra skirt. The woman flapped the cloth once or twice in the air in front of her and placed it over the mattress. Then she sat down again, settling herself on the mattress, her back against the back of the driver's cabin and her legs curled to one side. The giant leaned over and placed my groaning, shrouded mother onto the mattress with her head resting on the black woman's soft, generous lap.

The cabin doors on the Model-T had been removed and the huge Boer indicated that Rosemary-Ann and I should climb in. He leaned across us into the cabin and pumped the throttle several times before leaving it slightly pulled out, then walked to the front of the little lorry and with a single grunting jerk of the radiator crank handle the engine burst into discordant, shaking life.

Rosemary-Ann and I had seated ourselves on the slippery canvas seat and as the Model-T came to life the gearstick resting between Rosemary-Ann's right knee and my left commenced to vibrate so violently that its black knob became completely blurred and the entire driver's cabin started to shake. I grabbed onto Rosemary-Ann and we clung to each other as we too began to vibrate, the shaking cabin threatening to bounce us right back into the dusty street.

The giant climbed into the cabin and pushed the

throttle back into the rusty tin dashboard, whereupon the gear stick and the entire cabin settled down to a much more manageable shaking and rattling and jerky sort of putt-putting. In a cloud of blue smoke together with a brace of backfires, we moved away down the empty main street and into captivity.

I had stopped sniffling but continued to hang onto Rosemary-Ann who, weighed down with the responsibility of my mother and me, hadn't uttered a single word since we'd left the room behind the shop. Once in a while she'd sniff and jerk her head backwards so that her long blonde plaits bounced against her pretty face and a tear would run down her vibrating cheek and bounce over the edge, to disappear into the lap of her dirty printed cotton dress.

With Rosemary-Ann crying like that, I knew we must be in pretty big trouble all right — crying was not her game at all. The giant was so overwhelmingly in control that I guessed she, like me, must have become resigned to our fate as his dinner. Though, I must quickly add, I wasn't entirely without hope.

The thought of the black woman in the back cheered me up no end. In my book, evil giants didn't keep big, soft, smiling nannies on hand to cut up scrawny little children into eatable chunks. My commonsense told me that to a vicious and cruel giant she would be delicious herself and that he would have eaten her long since. There was, I told myself, definitely some room for hope.

———•———

We stayed on Oupa Winterbach's remote farm for more that six months, mixed up with the small sons and daughters of his sons and daughters, no different in any way to his own family.

The word *Oupa* simply means 'Grandfather' and, as he made no distinction between the two of us and his own grandchildren, it soon seemed perfectly natural to refer to him in this way. What I mean by this is that he ignored us all and let us run wild on the farm, allowing only that we should come back to the farmhouse for feeding purposes and to sleep.

Our lives were controlled by *Ousis*, a word which literally means 'older sister', but at the same time means much, much more. Ousis was almost as tall as Oupa Winterbach and probably weighed as much as him. She held absolute dominion over us kids.

Some hormonal irregularity had given her a pronounced moustache and she wore her dark hair pulled back and braided around her head. She walked around in bare feet, wearing a tentlike faded floral dress which seemed clean enough to my eyes but which she never seemed to change, or perhaps she had lots of them all the same.

Ousis had a *basso profondo* voice which would bring the little black kitchen maids trembling to her side from just about anywhere and when she brought her fingers to her lips and whistled we kids would come running and the bush doves in the blue gum trees would fly up in fright. But underneath all her fierceness was a heart as big as a tractor engine.

Ousis rose at four each morning to bake bread in the Dutch oven in the farmyard behind the kitchen. At five she woke the eleven kids who slept in the two brass Victorian feather beds in a large, dark room leading onto the back step. By the time we emerged into the kitchen, knuckling the sleep from our eyes, the scrubbed pine table was covered with tin mugs filled with steaming sweet mountain coffee beside which stood a large basket of rock-hard rusks, the result of a week's continuous baking in the autumn. The maids had long since smeared the kitchen floor with fresh cow dung which had dried to a soft khaki-yellow colour, so that each morning smelled of new cut grass and fresh baked bread.

It was Ousis who fed us and admonished us — though usually a telling-off concluded with a laugh — and it was she who nursed our cuts, painting them with iodine which stung like billyo. She also mended the tears in our ragged clothes and sometimes even patched up our quarrels.

At night we stood in line in the kitchen and in turn sat on a *riempie* stool and placed our dirty feet into a large tin basin of hot water while one of the maids, kneeling on the floor beside us, gave them a bit of a scrub with a coarse loofah brush. Then, from a separate basin of almost clean water, the maid wiped our hands and face with a warm cloth, separating our fingers and working the coarse towelling between them, squeezing out the dirt while being completely unmindful of cuts and sores and ignoring the winces and ouches and cries of indignation as we were practically murdered every night. After the agony of the hands we had to close our eyes while the dirt was wiped from our faces. Working a flannelled forefinger expertly, the maid would pry the dry, dusty snot from our noses.

Ousis made us kneel beside the two great brass beds and say our prayers before she tucked us in and turned the paraffin lamp down to a thin circle of orange light, sufficient only to soften the dark so that we would not be fearful of the night or, in our dreams, mistake the babble of the brook which ran past the open window for the cackling laughter of dead kaffir ghosts.

I would lie very still in the great feather bed under a mosquito net with five other kids asleep around me and listen. Soon, over the squabble of water, would come a different sound, the soughing of the wind through the huge old blue gum trees which surrounded the farmstead, a towering inferno of noise that swept and rushed and whooshed in a leafy kingdom two hundred feet above the hard, stamped earth of the farmyard. This was Jack and the Beanstalk Country all right, but Oupa Winterbach hadn't turned out to be even one bit as fearsome as a giant.

Though I have to say, life wasn't all that hot at first. I was the smallest of the eight boys on the farm and although I was learning Afrikaans pretty quickly, it wasn't nearly quick enough. I was a *rooinek*, which I soon learned wasn't a very good thing to be. I got beaten up when I didn't know a word in Afrikaans or made the mistake of asking for something in English. While being beaten up by the other kids was an extremely good incentive to learn a new language it wasn't doing my confidence much good in the meantime.

I recall one time, soon after we'd arrived on the farm, being circled by the other kids who laughed and made fun of me as I sat in the dirt bawling and sniffing through a bloody nose I'd received for a grammatical indiscretion. Suddenly, a great shadow fell over us and Ousis appeared and scooped me up in her arms and carried me some distance away. Finally, she sat her huge body, with me almost lost in her lap, on one of the steps leading up to the farmhouse. She didn't seem to mind that I dripped blood onto her skirt and she made no attempt to stop the flow.

'Come *skatterbol*, you are only five, this is the last time you may cry. You see, when you cry you make me cry also!' Whereupon Ousis burst into tears so violently that they splashed down her great red cheeks and crashed onto the back of my neck.

This lukewarm waterfall of grief seemed miraculously to stop the flow of blood from my nose and I immediately ceased crying, quite unable to compete with her Victoria Falls of blubbing.

'No, no, little *boetie*, you must cry some more!' she demanded between great, gulping sobs. 'This is the last time! After this you must never cry again. Your mama wrote to say tomorrow you are six, at six a man can't cry any more, you hear?'

Ousis gave another anguished sob, hugging me to her enormous breasts, and together we commenced to cry at the top of our voices. I'm telling you that was a cry and a half, but it soon became apparent that I'd quite suddenly grown out of crying, a day before it was supposed to happen.

On the day of our arrival at Oupa Winterbach's farm my mother was taken to Tzaneen hospital some thirty miles away. I don't remember her leaving us, I only remember that some time later, when she was well enough to leave hospital, she came to the farm to grow strong again. She was very thin and a bit dried out, with large black rings around her eyes. Ousis placed her in a second rocking chair under the blue gum trees to sit beside Oupa Winterbach's senile old wife, Ouma, who never spoke and seemed only to fumble with a brass snuff box from which she pinched snuff to her nostrils all day.

Ouma, which means 'grandma', was a sort of wheezing and sneezing machine, a tiny lady dressed in black who wore a shawl over her head. We weren't allowed to go too near her and I was to learn from the other children that she had gone mad in the Kaffir Wars because of what the kaffirs had done to her. What this was, was never explained, but it must have been something pretty terrible to send her wheezing and sneezing and mad all over the place like that.

Indeed, when you approached her she'd slowly turn her head and give a high, frightened cackle, shaking her bony finger in your direction. Then she'd bring her tiny white claws up and clutch fearfully at her breast and begin to whimper and sniff. 'She thinks you're a kaffir and are going to do it to her,' one of the other kids would explain, darkly, 'the kaffirs did it to her a hundred times in the Kaffir Wars, man!'

I was never able to discover what 'it' was, but if Ousis saw you teasing Ouma, or even going too close to the old woman, she'd give you such a solid clout behind the earhole that the force of her pile-driving arm would send you travelling several yards forward with your nose finally skidding in the dust. So we mostly stayed well away from the wheezing, constantly sneezing old crone who had it done to her a hundred times by filthy, black kaffirs.

In the case of Rosemary-Ann and I, this forbidden Ouma territory was very traumatic. My mother's recuperating presence next to the old lady made it impossible for us to approach her, except for a brief kiss at night when she always begged us in a thin, pleading voice which didn't sound at all like her old one, to be good and do as we were told because Oupa Winterbach was a precious man.

The other kids decided that because of her propin-quity with Ouma, she too must be mad and soon their taunting became so bad that I also believed this.

'Your ma is mad! Your ma is mad! Ha, ha, ha, you've got no pa and your ma is mad, mad, *mad!*' They'd circle around me like hyenas as I held my hands to my ears in a vain attempt to block these terrible words.

When they grew tired of taunting me, I'd wait until nobody was looking and go to a secret place I'd discov-ered, a small dark wattle and daub shed standing a little distance from the farmhouse. The dark, cool hut con-tained bags of mealie meal and from its open blue gum rafters hung large yellow leaves of tobacco and a few spikes of dry aloe, which was ground very fine and used as medicine mixed in Ouma's snuff. I loved the sweet smell from the tobacco tainted with the slightly musty odour that came from the bags of ground corn. It was a sort of comforting aroma that went well with the soft half-light and the business of being alone.

I'd sit on a plump bag of mealie meal, the coarse hessian scratching the backs of my knees, and try to control my feeling of helplessness at the demise of my mother from malaria into madness. I even wondered if when kaffirs did it, it first turned into malaria and then into madness. That perhaps unbeknown to us the kaffirs had done it to my mother, although she'd never spoken about being in a kaffir war. But when I asked Rosemary-Ann she said malaria came from mosquitoes.

I confess my concern for my mother was less than the anxiety over what would become of Rosemary-Ann and I if she was sent to the madhouse as the other kids promised she would be. I must admit, I was a bit of a worrier at the time and my mother sitting dozing in the shade in her rocking chair beside Ouma wasn't all that helpful a sight to one like me even though Ousis told me repeatedly that she was getting better and would soon be her old self again.

I should have had more confidence, for Ousis had proved quite right in another matter — apart from a few stray sniffs, I discovered that it was no longer possible for me to cry. So I'd just sit and worry a lot and have a bit of a sniff now and again and feel pretty miserable. But then I'd hear the sound of the railway sleeper that hung from the branch of an old plum tree outside the kitchen which Ousis used to hit with an iron rod to bring us kids in for lunch or dinner when she didn't feel like whistling. Life has a habit of going on.

In the weeks that followed my mother grew well again. But before we could get to know her again, she had to return to work in Duiwelskloof, the little town where we'd lived behind Mr Polanski's shop. My mother was to leave us on Winterbach's farm until she could afford to have us back with her again.

I must say, my mother's miraculous return to sanity (if she ever was mad) didn't please my playmates over-much; it was much more spooky having two mad women rocking under the blue gum trees. But, for my part, with my fears for my mother dispelled, life on the farm picked up a whole lot.

Now, more than fifty years later, the impressions of that time fold over each other in no particular sequence. My memory is of soon speaking Afrikaans as well as Shangaani. Of lowing red cattle mulling in a giant kraal formed of twisted, bone white wood. Of the papery rustle of wind through late summer corn.

Out of nowhere sometimes comes a memory of late

mornings, when the heat silenced even the singing of the women picking cotton and the shimmering, glassy air filled up so completely with the shrillness of cicadas that after a while you didn't hear them and their shrilling became the stillness itself. I can still recall the flat, dry smell of late afternoon heat and the dark, blurred shapes of returning cattle, the bells of the milking cows tinkling softly in the rapidly folding-down day, and the cries of greeting from the half-seen shapes of naked herd boys in a cloud of beast dust, backlit against a blood red bush-veldt sunset.

But of all these memories there is one; one single incident which changed my life forever. Let me tell you about the Monkey Man.

Near Oupa Winterbach's farm lies the royal kraal of Mojadji, the rain queen. She belonged to the Venda tribe, a people who have never in their history made war on any other tribe and who have only one purpose in life, to bring to their throne a queen who is placed on Earth with the greatest of all the powers; the power to make rain.

Nobody knows where these rain people came from. They were thought to have been born near the misty conjunction of two great rivers when time was an infant and where the gods, who made them especially beautiful and pure, gave them the gift of rain to protect them from the marauding tribes sweeping down from the north. The rain queen and her people lived under the protection of all the tribes. Even the Boers, who had known drought often enough, were not prepared to defame her magic powers. Too many times beyond coincidence they'd heard the royal drums of Mojadji beat out their commands to a brazen, barren sky and often before nightfall it was filled with heavy, dark rain clouds veined with lightning and growling with the most promising of thunder.

There was an unspoken rule among the tribes that Mojadji could only be visited after the dust devils had ridden for three spring seasons across parched lands and only after the *Sangomas*, great and small, had exhausted their own powers to make rain. This they would do by casting the bones and lighting a magic fire, watching as the sacred smoke rises up into a sky shorn of its fleece of clouds by the angry gods. When, day after day, month after month, despite their powerful incantations and magic spells the sky still stretched above their thirsty lands, smooth and blue as skimmed milk, only then would they pack away the knuckle bones of the sacred white ox and admit that their power was not enough to break open the blue shell of a recalcitrant sky.

'It is time to go to her, only she can reach the gods now and please them with her voice and beauty and cunning female ways,' they would tell the chiefs and tribal elders.

Then they would begin to make preparations for the journey to the north to make a supplication to Mojadji, the greatest of all women, whose throne sat on a great golden cloud which only a *Sangoma* who had prepared his rituals correctly could see with magic eyes.

The people of the tribe would understand that this particular drought, this particular sky, could only be broken if their witchdoctor chose his omens carefully and arrived at the royal kraal of Mojadji at the propitious time, when the day moon was full and white in the sky. Only then and after supplication to the rain queen would the drums of Mojadji begin to beat, their rhythm picked up and repeated exactly, to the very shadow of a single beat, by the drums of the other tribes, until finally they reached the parched lands of the supplicant tribe, even a thousand miles away.

Soon puffs like early morning breath would appear. Then cotton clouds strung across the horizon like herds of grazing pure white goats, after which would follow great towering cliffs and mountains of tumbling air filled with moisture. Often, on the very day given by the great queen, the rains came, great splashes that struck down at an angle and smacked into the earth and kicked up the dust then roared into a positive fury, turning the parched soil into roiling red mud to be carried thundering down dry creek beds, the rushing, gorgeous blood of Mojadji's generous gift.

In the respect of rain, it was known from the beginning of time that her power was greater by far than the greatest of witchdoctors. Men, whose power as soothsayers and healers held tens of thousands of people in awe, would kneel humbly at the feet of the young queen and speak with respect in a voice never above a hoarse whisper. The Monkey Man had come to do the same, for the clouds had not gathered for three seasons above the peaks and *kranse* of the high Drakensberg and there was a great and lingering drought in Zululand.

The Monkey Man, who I learned from the kitchen maids was a powerful and famous witchdoctor, must somehow have been known to Oupa Winterbach or perhaps he was summoned; all I know is that he appeared on the farm on an afternoon two days after a terrible crisis had occurred.

A four-gallon tin of paraffin and a hurricane lamp had been stolen from the storehouse behind the kitchen. This was an unthinkable thing to happen; nothing on the farm

was ever locked. Stealing was simply unimaginable, and
the punishment, therefore, could also be worse than the
mind could ever dream of. Nevertheless, the paraffin and
the lamp were missing and while all the servants and
farm labourers were paraded outside the house and the
thief given until morning to replace the stolen goods,
nothing as yet had happened.

It was also inconceivable that someone other than a
farm labourer or servant was responsible; no strange
African would be able to put a foot on the property
without being spotted. The culprit, we gathered from the
grown-ups, was definitely some *verdomde kaffir* on the farm
who was already dead meat.

The Monkey Man drove up in a 1936 Buick, a vehicle
which denoted his status as one of the great witchdoctors
of Africa as well as a man of enormous wealth. But in
this part of the world it counted for little. He was still a
kaffir, a heathen, a child of evil and a nobody, less even
than a nobody, because he was made by the devil and
created in the likeness of an ageing monkey.

Which was perfectly true. The great witchdoctor was
less than four foot high with a pronounced hump on his
back and so old that his stoop brought his head almost
to his knees. His arms hung apelike as he walked and he
seemed to constantly mutter and jabber. The old man's
hair and beard were snowy white and grew in a great
fuzzy bush around his tiny simian face which featured
rheumy eyes so red that they appeared the colour of
diluted blood.

To me he was a frightening sight and I didn't hesitate
to believe in his awesome powers. He may have been just
a dirty old kaffir, but he wasn't the sort you went around
throwing stones at. He wore the traditional leopard skin

which hung from his shoulders to the ground and carried a beautifully beaded fly-switch of horse hair. He would turn his head constantly from side to side as he walked, a quick little jerk, his expression suspicious, taking everything in, even though his head seemed no more than a couple of feet above the ground and he had to look up even at me.

I felt certain he could look directly into my wicked, frightened heart and putting his tiny black claw through my chest, tear it out and examine it, sniff it, shake his head in disgust and jabbering, throw it into the dust at his feet. For even at my young age I felt a guilt, a guilt of skin and guilt for my blue eyes and the way I was expected to perceive the dark people around me.

That night the little black kitchen maids who washed our feet and hands told us that Oupa Winterbach had paid the great *umNgoma* to find out who had stolen the paraffin and the hurricane lamp. The whites of their eyes showed large and astonished as they talked of this, knowing that it was impossible for the culprit to escape the trap the mighty *umNgoma* would set for him. The Monkey Man's powers they said were so great that the thief was utterly and completely doomed and would surely die, possibly even before morning and even without the great witchdoctor laying a finger on him or even seeing him face to face.

Late the following morning, in the extreme heat of the day, all the servants and farm labourers were paraded outside the farmhouse. Oupa Winterbach stood watching with his great *sjambok*, tapping the thick, malevolent looking five-foot plaited leather whip impatiently against his moleskins while the Monkey Man screeched at all the male Africans to stand in a straight line in front of him.

When they finally stood in a more or less straight line
the Monkey Man ordered them to extend their left arm
from the elbow, palm upward. This done, the tiny wizard
hopped from one black man to the next, taking a tiny
pebble from a leather bag tied around his neck and,
stretching up, placed it onto the palm of each outstretched hand.

We all watched, anxious to see whether a particular
hand would begin to shake with guilt as the magic pebble
started to vibrate or glow red hot, burning a sizzling,
flesh-popping hole right through the hand. But soon so
many hands were shaking in terror at the mere prospect
of being accused that this was obviously not a method
that could possibly discover the culprit.

Next the Monkey Man built a tiny fire of grass and
chicken feathers, sprinkling it with a powder that made
the flames turn blue and flare up and made the smoke
rising from the fire into a thin, dense white column. He
waved his hands through the smoke as though he was
gathering it up then rubbed the invisibly captured smoke
into his face, his tiny tongue darting in and out rapidly as
he licked at the air in front of him, making a strange
high-pitched sound of the kind you might expect to hear
from a ghost.

After a minute or so, when the fire had died down, he
patted the ashes and spread them into a circle about two
feet in diameter. Seated on his haunches, he withdrew
the shin bones of the great white ox from an ancient
leather bag which hung separately around his neck and
tossed them, one at a time, so that they each landed with
a tiny explosion of dust and ash within the circle.

He sat watching the bones, from time to time groaning and keening as he rocked on his haunches, then he

would flick suddenly at one of them, sending it spinning out of the circle. Growling and chattering to himself he'd hop over to where it landed, watch it carefully for a moment then pounce on it, scoop it up and swallow it, shaking his head as the marble-sized bone disappeared like a worm down a chicken's throat. Finally, with all the bones inside his stomach, he rose and moved over to a chicken, which lay a short distance away with its legs trussed. He produced a pocket-knife from the same leather bag which had contained the pebbles; it was an old knife with a mottled celluloid mother-of-pearl handle of the kind you could buy at any kaffir store very cheaply. Holding the chicken by the head, its beak clasped shut in his tiny paw, he stood over the circle and slit its throat above the ashes, the bright drops of blood splashing onto the shiny breast feathers of the wildly fluttering bird before spraying a shower of crimson droplets.

Finally, when the chicken had stilled to an occasional convulsive jerk he swung it in an arch several times, then released it, hurling it over his shoulder. The chicken's head remained in his hand as the carcase flew high into the air with the blood spouting from its open throat, clearly spotting two of the Africans standing in line.

There was a loud moan as the chicken landed lifeless in the dust, then all eyes turned to look at the two men who had been spotted with chicken blood. Their faces started to crumble and their teeth began to chatter, their bodies to shake violently. One of them started to howl like a jackal, a grown man bawling his head off. But neither moved from the line, their hands still containing the tiny pebble held shaking in front of them.

The Monkey Man dropped the chicken's head inside the circle, turned slowly and, in Shangaani, shouted so all could hear his shrill voice. I was now beginning to understand the language quite well, it is not so very far removed from Zulu which I'd learned at my nanny's breast. Roughly translated, this is what he said to the two blood-splattered men.

'You two are too stupid to be the thieves, the blood has marked you innocent. You may step out of the line.' Turning away from the two men whom we had all felt certain must be guilty, the Monkey Man looked at the remaining farm labourers and started to cackle, his few remaining teeth wet and yellow in his mouth.

'Ha! Your hands have stopped shaking. When you saw the blood land on your brothers you gained courage, but it is among you, not them, that I will find the guilty person!'

Almost immediately several hands began to shake all over again and the old man, pointing his finger in the direction of the line of men, ran it slowly down to include them all.

'Your fear is indecent, but then you are only of the Shangaan people, so you are born cowards whose mothers made love to hyenas so now you can eat only the flesh that the Zulu lion has blooded and killed for you.'

A moan of despair came from the men who were already in a deep state of fear and shock. The Monkey Man looked again at the two men who'd been blooded by the chicken and who now stood two paces or so out of the line. 'Go, be off with you!' he screeched. The two Africans, turning their backs on us, ran for their lives, quickly disappearing into a field of ripe mealies where we could hear them, in a desperate attempt to make a quick getaway, crashing willy-nilly among the dry corn stalks.

Oupa Winterbach and the other grown-ups and of course us kids thought this was very funny and laughed a lot. Even I could see the joke. Despite their own fear some of the black men in the line started to laugh, though I couldn't see what they had to laugh about, they were up to their eyeballs in trouble.

The little witchdoctor started to cackle as well, hopping from one leg to another in a crazy jig, holding his hands on his hips. He laughed and laughed, his shrill cackle growing higher and higher until all the whites stopped laughing and watched him, bemused. Then, as suddenly as he'd started, he stopped and walked stiff-legged over to the circle containing the chicken head and blood mixed with the ash from his magic fire.

Straddling the circle, he bent low so that his face was only about eight inches from the ground and one after another the knuckle bones of the great white ox fell from his mouth and rolled into a perfect circle all on their own, surrounding the chicken head. Its once beady eyes were now shut in death by deep purple eyelids, and tiny sugar ants were already crawling around it's half-open beak.

The Monkey Man now began to dance around the circle. As though he was playing a game of marbles, he'd stop suddenly and flick at a tiny bone, sending it shooting at high speed, bouncing and running in the dirt in the direction of the black men. He continued doing this until all the tiny shin bones lay scattered across the line of Africans.

We all instantly understood the ploy. Where the bones landed would be the guilty ones. But we were wrong again. The Monkey Man raised himself as high as he could given his stooped back and with his hands on his hips announced, 'You must have no fear, only they who are guilty will be found. The tasting of the pebble will make you innocent. I will come to each of you and as I do you will put the pebble you hold in your mouth, suck it a moment and then spit it back into my hand.'

He walked to the end of the row farthest from where we stood and each African did as instructed, first placing the pebble in his mouth then, after a moment, spitting it into the witchdoctor's tiny outstretched claw stained with the blood from the chicken. As each pebble landed in his palm the old man would examine it briefly before dropping it onto the dust at his feet, whereupon he would say '*ngazi luTho olubi*', declaring the spitter innocent.

The pressure was unbearable. Nearly three-quarters of the way along the line he examined a pebble in his hand then suddenly snatched at the ragged shirt of the young African man in front of him, pulling him from the line. The boy, for he was hardly yet a man, immediately dropped to his knees, quivering all over as he cowered in the dust, his face cupped in his hands.

The Monkey Man seemed hardly to notice him and continued along the line, accepting and examining each pebble as it landed in his hand. A little further on he repeated the snatch, pulling a second young man from the line. He too dropped to the ground and began to howl for mercy, pointing to the first young man, sobbing that he'd made him do it.

Finally, the Monkey Man came to the end of the line and walked away without saying a word or even glancing at Oupa Winterbach or the two young black men grovelling and snivelling in the dust. They'd both started to grab handfuls of dust which they threw over their heads,

so that their peppercorn hair and faces were soon covered in red dust.

Oupa Winterbach commanded the two guilty boys to
approach him and they rose and moved to where he
stood, cowering at his feet. He bent down and ripped
the ragged shirts from their backs then, rising, drew his
sjambok lightly over their naked spines so that they
twitched in fright. He asked them quietly in Shangaani
where the stolen paraffin and lamp were hidden. The
two young men rose to their knees, bringing their hands
together in front of their faces and, with their bodies
shaking uncontrollably, they told him.

Oupa Winterbach placed his boot in turn on the
shoulder of each man at his feet and pushed him over so
that he sprawled in the dirt and lay still, not daring to
move, though the hopeless weeping of each one could be
heard by all of us. The huge Boer, leaving the culprits
where they lay, walked several paces from them and
commenced to speak to the remaining Africans. His
voice seemed somehow different to the one he used on
the farm. Now a booming, stertorous sound came from
his bearded mouth, as though he was a great prophet,
like Elijah preaching the wrath of God.

'You are the devil's children, the sons of Ham!' He
turned to indicate the whites who stood slightly behind
him. 'And we are the sons and daughters of the Father
of Heaven.' He ran his finger down the line of men, his
eyes taking each one in. 'It is not possible for you to steal
from us, you hear? Escape from our punishment, from
God's punishment, cannot be. I am not mocked, sayeth
the Lord!'

Then his voice changed down a gear, though at the
same time it seemed to grow more angry. 'You all know

I will not call the police. We will not have the police on this farm so that my good name is associated with kaffirs who steal!' He spat into the dust at his feet. 'Who steal the bread from my table! I will not permit this shame upon my people. I will punish these devil kaffirs myself, you hear?'

There was a groan from the long line, but many of the black heads shook in agreement. Oupa Winterbach turned to us and sighed, speaking in an almost sad voice, 'It is God's will and God's way.' Then he turned, addressing Ousis. 'Take the women away and the girls too, let the men and boys stay, they must see how God's justice works.'

He waited until the women had returned to the farm-house, then Oupa Winterbach walked over to the first African and, grabbing him by the leather strap which held his ragged trousers, he lifted the man from the ground and carried him forward so that all the Africans present could see him. He dropped him on his stomach over an old sawn-off blue gum stump, so that his right hand hung from the side of the stump and the remainder of his torso and left hand lay spread upon it, his legs hanging down over the end.

The young African's slender black body occupied only half of the great stump. Oupa Winterbach returned to the second African and, clasping him up in the same manner, dropped him too onto the smooth flat stump so that his left arm hung from its opposite side, his dark knuckles touching the ground. Then he lifted the left and right arms of the two Africans and crossed them so that the two men lying on their bellies had their arms around the top half of each other's back.

Oupa Winterbach went to work with the *sjambok*,

landing it expertly, cutting it deep into the shoulder joint of first the one crossed black arm and then the other. The force of his blows echoed among the gum trees as the whip cut through the skin and layer of fat into the flesh, ripping it open, exposing the gristle and finally the shoulder joints. The giant stopped only when the *sjambok* had cut through the flesh and sinew and smashed apart the shoulder joints of both arms, leaving bloody stumps where the arms had once been joined to the top of the shoulders.

Both men were unconscious long before this happened. The blue gum stump was splashed all over and the hard earth at its base was crimson with their blood. Nobody stirred in the line of black men, nor did any of the whites move from where they stood.

Only I, the weak-stomached *rooinek*, was unable to contain my horror and long before it was over I had run away to my secret place when I lay retching, my body spread over a sack of mealie meal. I lay very still, very frightened, my heart beating like a frightened bird and then I experienced a warm feeling around my crotch and realised that I'd pissed my pants. The piss, draining through the hessian, soaked into the mealie meal inside.

I had seen the *sjambok*, the five-foot-long fierce, serpent of leather land with the weight and fury of a seven-foot, three-hundred-pound giant behind it. I had watched trembling as it split flesh, blood splashing over and bits of human flesh clinging to Oupa Winterbach's moleskins until they were soaked from his waist to his knees. I was never to forget that single moment when the first of a hundred or maybe a thousand cuts of the *sjambok* landed and I observed the crimson flash of flesh torn open on a human back.

When I decided to find a new land as far from Africa as it was possible to run, I carried with me the memory of two dark severed arms left to lie on the blood-soaked tree stump after Ousis had ordered the unconscious bodies of the two men brought to her so that she could stem the blood and clean the ragged shoulder stumps before the heat and flies caused unnecessary infection. For me those two severed arms, laid out on a blood-soaked, make-shift butcher's block, has always been the true symbol of apartheid.

———

How long I lay in the dark cool shed I cannot say, but I had taken off my pants and spread them on a sack of mealies to dry and then seated myself naked on an adjacent sack, my eyes closed, the terrible *sjambok* sound still in my head and down my throat and deep into my guts where it echoed worse even than the echoes of the blue gum trees.

After a while I became aware that I was not alone. I opened my eyes to see the Monkey Man sitting on his haunches some few feet away looking at me. 'They tell me you speak Zulu, white boy?'

I nodded, terrified, covering my scrotum at the sight of the tiny black man.

'Then you and I will speak Zulu. You are not of the *amabhunu*, the Boer, for you cry for the wrong skin?'

He looked directly at my covered private parts. 'Take away your hands, this is not a part to shame you, there is no shame in being naked, all Zulu *umfana* at your age are naked, it is how they should be, it is proper.'

It was an instruction to be obeyed and I quickly removed my hands. 'Yes, you are not *amabhunu*,' he said again, looking at my circumcised penis. I nodded, admitting that I wasn't a Boer, my eyes wide with fear.

'I have thrown the bones and I have seen you in the smoke and now I must teach you where to hide so that when you are afraid or lack courage you can go to where you can still the fear and be brave again.' He pulled his head to one side, looking at me through his bloodshot eyes. 'Will you listen to me, white boy?'

I had not heard Zulu spoken since we'd left Natal when I'd lost my beautiful big nanny, at a time, long ago, when the world had been a safe place for our family. The words spoken by the Monkey Man were in her language and she had never done anything to me that wasn't good. I nodded to the old man, beginning to lose a little of my fear.

'Ha! I think you are a white Zulu,' he laughed. He held up his fly-switch, the handle of which was embroidered in an elaborate pattern of tiny coloured beads. 'Watch!' He grasped the fly-switch by the horse hair so that the brightly beaded handle hung down. Slowly he began to swing the handle like a pendulum. 'Watch the beads, watch them sway like an old woman's buttocks,' he cackled and then continued, 'Sway, sway, watch them sway as she goes on her way. Sway, sway, sway . . .' His voice was growing slower and lower. 'She goes to gather water in a great clay pot sway, sway, sway, to cook her husband mealie pap and serve it steaming hot! Sway, sway, sway. Now count aloud the number of all your fingers on both your hands. Sway, sway, sway . . .'

I began to count to ten. 'No, slowly, count slowly and when you reach ten close your eyes, but slowly,' he instructed.

I began to count again, watching the sweep of the

handle which was now a soft blur of colour in front of my eyes. My eyelids seemed to grow heavy, reaching ten I closed them gratefully. 'Now count to ten again, but this time backwards. When you reach the number of one you will be asleep little white man who mourns at the blood from a black man's back. You will be in the night country.'

I began to count down from ten but I don't recall if I ever made it back to one.

'See now how you sit at the mouth of a dark cave and overlook this place. If you look beyond it, look into the far distance beyond your sight, you will see the great water. The great water that rests beyond the Limbombo Mountains. It is the time of the setting sun. Now you see the sun as it enters into the great dark wetness, its golden fire quenched. Now see again, it is gone only a moment and immediately it begins to rise again, see how it rises silver from the water, the moon over the night country. It is here you can come whenever you are sad or frightened. It is here where you can rethink your courage and find the way to go and the path to take. It is here where you can meet your *shades* and speak to them. They are the spirits of your ancestors, they will be your guides.'

I could hear his voice clearly as I sat cross-legged outside a small cave. Below me stretched Oupa Winterbach's farm. I could hear the swoosh and the fury of the wind through the blue gum trees and see the small, dark shape of Ouma in her rocking chair. Then I looked further beyond the bone white kraal and across the corn fields . . . I seemed to lose the sight of my eyes and a new landscape grew inside my head.

Stretching away from me was a dark, flat watery firmament that filled the entire space in front of me, as though I was suspended directly in line with the horizon. As the old man spoke a great fiery orb dropped from above my line of sight and plunged into the ink-dark line, like a bright new copper penny dropped into the slot of a money box. There was no splash, no sound at all, simply a huge golden orb disappearing into the black line etched against a barely lighter sky.

Almost immediately I could see it begin to rise from the water. The world around me filled with a light almost as clear as daylight and below me the farm again appeared, bathed in moonlight, the shadows of the trees splashed across the settled dust of the farmyard, the glint of the brook crossing it. But no farmhouse. Oupa Winterbach's home was gone. In its place, rising out of the red dust, were two black arms ending in fists clenched to the sky and beyond them I could see the great blue gum stump, its silver grey colour washed clean, as though it were some once-upon-a-time sacrificial altar now used only by the ghosts of men long since past.

'You may come back here whenever you wish by closing your eyes and sitting very still and by counting to ten, frontways and backways. This place will always be yours little white boy who has tears enough for a black man's mourning.'

His voice faded and I opened my eyes to find I was alone in the cool, dark shed, seated cross-legged on top of a bag of mealie meal, my hands quietly in my lap. I could smell the pungent tobacco leaf hanging from the rafter above me. It was mixed with the slightly damp, musty smell of the crushed corn. Outside I heard the solitary *schwark* of a hen complaining to herself about the noonday heat.

I never again saw the Monkey Man and I was too afraid to ask when he'd departed in his big black Buick.

Had it not been for the discovery that night as I lay in bed listening as I always did to the wind beyond the water, that by following his simple instructions I could return to the night country, I may have come to think that his coming to me in the shed was simply an imagined thing brought about by my hysteria.

Years later, when I'd won a scholarship to a posh boys' school well beyond the means of our family, I was mucking around in the biology lab library late one afternoon, leafing through a book on human behaviour for an essay I had to write, when I finally worked out the magic of the Monkey Man. I realised how he had unerringly picked the two thieves who would each lose an arm in the name of the white man's God, a white man's truth and a white man's justice.

Fear had completely dried up the saliva in the mouths of the two guilty men. The pebbles they spat into the Monkey Man's tiny claw were the only two which were completely dry. Fear is like that, it starts in a dry mouth and it works its way down through the inside of a man and everything it touches it dries up, so that finally even the soul shrivels away and a man, consumed by fear, is as good as dead.

Dough

———◆———

SARA DOWSE

In the shtetl where Ruchel Kozminsky lived and worked and waited for her husband, there was a clock. It had been installed in the sixteenth century, when the province was still a part of Poland, and it stood in its carved wooden tower in the centre of the town's market square. The town had prospered under the benevolent rule of the local noble, who had pressed the peasants into producing grain and cattle for export, and he himself had commissioned the tower. Carpenters built it from thick planks of oak, and the clock, with its cast-iron bell that struck the hour, was imported from England. The town, too, was constructed entirely of native timbers, and as such was subject to frequent fires; and in the middle of the following century Cossacks led by the infamous

Bohdan Chmielnicki burned it down. But wood was plentiful in the region and such was the shtetl's spirit that within two years it was rebuilt completely, including the synagogue and the nobleman's clock.

It was the first thing that Ruchel saw when she came at dawn to set up her stall. The tower, with its straight sides and pointed, pyramid shape at the top, would be licked by a rosy, golden light that reminded her of flames, and it seemed as though the clock had indeed stopped and was at that very moment being consumed by Chmielnicki's fire. She would give a little shudder, adjust her kerchief and set to work, balancing the timber slab on the trestles, snapping out the starched white cloth and letting it drift down onto her table, unwrapping her hot braided breads and placing them in artful piles on the cloth.

Through the day, as the sun grew hotter, and her mind grew tired of the chatter of the marketplace, she would find herself staring at the clock again. At midday, when the bell gave out twelve deep, clanging reverberations, the shadowless tower seemed as squat and smug as the local nobleman, the drunken descendant of the man who had commissioned the original. It was as if time itself had lost its soul, that Keteb, the noonday devil, had stolen it; and, as if to confirm this, the face of the clock, too, seemed to have lost all expression. Ruchel blinked, she was losing her mind with loneliness: it was all superstition, Lev had told her so.

And yet, and yet. There were many things she did not understand. When she was younger she thought that time was like the day, the early sunlight climbing over the horizon like honey pouring onto the land and then the sun rising higher and burning brighter in the sky and falling at last like a molten ball singeing the boughs of the pine trees on the hills. And the days became years, circular in their seasons; the hard frosts of winter melting into the mud and slush of the thaw, the sudden thrust of mountain springs and the joyful babble of the birds. Then came the flocks of new rabbits chasing through the thickets and next the tall bending grasses of summer and autumn's blanket of leaves. And she saw all the ages since creation spiralling, uncoiling, circles within circles tumbling towards her, time like the spinning spokes of wheels, or the hands of the clock in the tower before her, slowly extending its shadow across the square.

The year was marked also by the feasts, the grand cyclical procession of holy days. Thus it had been, for centuries, until one year there was a tumult, far away in France, and time shot forth like a comet, and everything, forever, was changed.

As a rule, girls and women were not to know of this. As a matter of fact, for many of the old people the Haskalah, the Enlightenment, was a curse, a blight, a plague, for men and women alike, to be stamped out as the worst form of trayf. But only the most pious were immune. All men are born, and remain, free and equal, the Frenchmen said, and this was to include the Jews. Into every far-flung ghetto and shtetl this notion crept, to some like a stealthy demon. What Ruchel had learned she had learned from Lev Kozminsky, the quiet, fervent scholar from Vilna. Litvaks were known to be sceptics, but this one seemed to gobble up uncritically everything he read. It was not that he would abandon the Torah, he told her, but that things from now on would be different — in the wider world a Jew could command respect. And she had thought that though he was naive and foolish, for even in the marketplace it was easy enough to see the respect that Christians had for Jews, his words stirred something inside her, something like a dim ancient memory whose precise delineations she could not yet grasp, and which frightened her for that very reason. But she went ahead and married him, in spite of her fears and the knowledge that though he would want her to leave with him she would not go, and even then she was fearful, not that he was wrong but that he might be right. So who was the more stubborn, he or she?

At the end of the day Ruchel shook out the crumbs from her tablecloth, folded it into a square, slipped it into the basket with the money she had earned, dismantled her trestle table and began the slow, weary, market-day trundle home. Her youngest daughter, Zipporah, was there to greet her when she got to the gate of the house, and Ruchel propped the table and the trestles against the gateposts and embraced her, worrying as she did that her thoughts were making her absent and aloof. For it seemed sometimes that she was all alone in the town when in fact not a day went by when she was not surrounded by people. Her mother, her father, her sisters, her friends, were all dear to her, so much so that she couldn't imagine a life without them, but for all her resisting it was clear that her marriage to the stubborn Vilna chachem had set her apart. And even as she was thinking this Zipporah was telling her of the letter that had arrived, was dancing about her, begging her to hurry inside and open it so they all would hear the news.

Dearest Ruchele,

Last week I bought a horse, a little spotted mare, not young but in reasonable condition, and a cart in which I am able to transport many more items than before. Out

*here in the west there are not many landsmen but the
farmers are good customers. Pots, pans, boxes, bottles and
cloth are popular — I get bolts of flannels and a tough-
wearing denim from Des Moines. The farmers give me a
bed but tonight I am lying in the cart, reading and
writing under the stars with the help of a kerosene
lantern. It is better for studying this way. The sky seems
very low and bright with stars, this is what I notice, the
vast expanse of it, that is at the same time close . . .*

It was then that the eldest, Miriam, cried: 'Oy, there are
Red Indians out there!'

Her brother Carl kicked her and laughed. 'Stupid!
Des Moines is the capital, a city.'

'It is only at night that he studies?' asked Ruchel's
mother.

When she had finished reading Ruchel laid the pages
in her lap. She shook her head. 'Does he need to work,
with me as provider?'

'He's saving for us, Mama,' Zipporah said. 'To take
us to America.'

'How much does a yeshiva bucher save?' grumbled
Ruchel's father.

Ruchel lifted her burning gaze from her lap. 'I will
write at once and tell him to come back.'

All this running, scurrying over the globe. She looked
around her, at her two frail parents and the dirty faces of
her children and felt secure. This was home, where she
could feed her family, bless the candles, bake her bread.
If part of her knew it for a dream, that it all could go up
in a moment's rush of flames, and whispered like Lev's
voice in the night that she must flee, then this is the part

that most frightened her, and she would pay it no heed.

The good thing was that everyone needed bread. Not only the fine white challah for Shabbes but the coarser, weekday varieties, the pumpernickels and ryes. In theory, every woman could bake her own, but not everyone did when Ruchel was around. Some had too many children, some had too many clothes to sew, another might have had too much work in her dairy. Others were too old, or too poor, and in summer perhaps the fear of fire kept some from running their stoves throughout the day. Only Ruchel could have told me for sure. Of course, I didn't know her well, and didn't think to ask her when I did. But one thing is clear. It was not at all unusual for a woman to earn money in a shtetl. It was needed, it was expected; it was tradition.

So, with the children scrambling around her and the old people grumbling in the corner Ruchel tended her oven and kneaded her dough, except in the summer months when she would work when they were sleeping and it was cool. In the deep silent dark of the morning she would wake with the chimes of the nobleman's clock, creep with her candle into the kitchen where Zipporah was still fast asleep, arrange the pile of kindling in the stove, setting larger, slower burning chunks on top of that, set the mass of it alight, and begin the expert process of sifting, mixing, kneading and shaping for which she was praised far and wide.

If you have done it yourself you would know that there is something deeply soothing in the simple, humble act of making bread. You take the flour and shake it through the sifter or a sieve. You take the yeast, dry or caked, and crumble it into the tepid water, mixing it with the sugar or molasses and salt and oil. Now you add some flour (no need to be exact), then some more. You beat the dough, add more flour and then, when by touch you sense that it all has reached the requisite pitch of elasticity, you begin the marvellous business of kneading. An ancient art, it can have the same effect as gazing at the moon and stars, a sensation of having transcended the boundaries of space and time. I have known people to take up breadmaking suddenly, unexpectedly, at crucial moments in their lives: a man who started after breaking up with his wife, a bank teller who taught herself to make croissants on receiving a promotion. I suspect it is due largely to the kneading. They say, in the utilitarian, instrumental fashion peculiar to Sunday supplements, that it's a means of releasing tension, all the wrapping and squeezing and folding and punching, and the man who'd divorced his wife claimed that he was only doing to the dough what he had regularly done to her breasts. But now that I know Ruchel's story I believe that dough can be more than just a device for assuaging hungers, sexual as well as visceral, although with Lev away for such long stretches at a time, there could have been something of that for her too. But still, there was more, definitely more; deeper, and different.

This particular summer night was in the middle of the week, so Ruchel was not making the light, slippery, oily dough for challah. Her recipe called for a thick grainy dough that required a good deal more kneading — at least fifteen minutes, and probably two or three extra spurts of five minutes each. Moreover, this dough was a sticky dough, which made the kneading that much harder again. In the winter she welcomed the labour and, besides, the children would often pitch in, to fold, push and turn and fold, push and turn, and their squabbling over who would do it next and for how long as least gave her muscles a rest and broke the monotony, and if Lev was home he would sometimes take over. But here, in the dark, aside from the sleeping Zipporah, Ruchel was alone, and as she worked her fingers and the heels of her hands into the tacky dough, her thoughts circled aimlessly, like the gnats bobbing and spinning in the waving air above the candle, and she began to think of time again, and space, because I suppose of the very great distance that lay between her and her husband. She pictured the stars above him in the farmers' fields, and the warm steady glow of his lamp, and the greater her concentration on these the more she sensed that the distance was really nothing, if time, as her thoughts, could stop circling, to move straight and clean like a silvery comet through the sky. And she imagined him, her sweet yeshiva bucher, her luftmensch, lying with the Torah in his cart, and it was as if she were actually there, lying in the straw beside him. She pressed the heels of her floury hands harder into the dough, then, relaxing the muscles of her arms, lifted the furthest end of it off the table and folded it once more into the middle, rocking with such force she might have been davening as she did.

And after several more minutes of this the world seemed plunged in silence, out of which a low, humming, buzzing noise began to slowly gather strength, blotting out any visual register of her surroundings: the rough, smoke-darkened walls, the packed earth of the floor, the black flaking iron of the stove, her sleeping child, the worn, scrubbed wood of the table where she worked. Ruchel squeezed the dough, gripping it now in her sweating palms as the trance seemed to grip her soul. The buzzing got louder, a shriek that bounced off the bones

of her skull. Was she being possessed? Had a demon —
a dybbuk — jumped inside her? But no, she was neither
agitated nor raving. She was calm, peaceful — the only
disturbing thing was the noise. And that too, gott zu
danken, was fading now. She was only vaguely aware of
her hands on the dough and the yeasty fragrance rising
up from it. Ahead was a swirl of stars; it was as though
they were spinning through a tunnel, or perhaps it was
she who was spinning; it was hard to know.

After a second or so, maybe less, the dizziness stopped,
and ahead she could see a wide, green land, green everywhere, with tall leafy plants coated with silvery drops of
dew, and all this under a bright hard sky a dense, vibrant
shade of blue. She could feel herself enter, the broad
leaves sprinkling moisture in her face as she brushed
against them in passing, the soles of her boots sinking
deep into the black, spongy earth. The buzzing that
assaulted her before was now the singing of pearly winged
insects, and the warmth of the sun high in the blue
overhead caressed her as she walked. She saw, in the near
distance, what appeared to be the skyline of an enormous
city, a city of ziggurats and onion domes, which glittered
and shimmered in the sunlight cascading from the sky;
and it seemed like no time at all before she had entered
the gates and was surrounded by these fabulous golden
constructions. And at her feet were cobblestones, so
smooth and so clean that they glowed, and when she
looked again she saw that they too were gold, just as she
had heard from the storytellers who visited the village.
So this is what Lev has been drawn to, she whispered,
sucking in her breath — America, El Dorado, the goldena medina! So beautiful, so foreign that she was more
afraid than she'd ever been.

But then, her eyes, at first quizzical, then wide with a grateful wonder, as if she were relieved that in all this beautiful strangeness there was still something familiar, something that she, a humble woman, might understand, she saw a clock. A clock like the nobleman's clock and yet, not like it, different in one or two arresting respects, but similar enough to make her feel, well, at least partially at ease. The clock had its tower, though needless to say this tower of solid gold had a dazzle altogether different from the dawn-kissed oak of the tower in the market square. And her heart gave a kick when she saw that the clockface had no hands — yet the crenellated tower cast a shadow, odd, she thought, with a noonday sun so high in the gleaming sky.

Her eye, following the line of this shadow, laid like a dark velvet cloth over the phosphorescent ripples of the cobblestones, almost overlooked what was central to the picture. A woman, an astonishingly beautiful woman, whose beauty Ruchel was unable to compare with anything she had ever seen. Her hair: what can I tell you about her hair? By what means could I describe it? Well, it was the deep, red, tawny colour of the woods in autumn, an intense, lustrous scarlet speckled and streaked with gold, and it spread over her majestic shoulders in a fury of waves and curls. Her lips were the darkest crimson, her skin was as pale and luminous as pearls. She wore a mantle embroidered with them, and lapis lazuli studded here and there, so that the vestment had the sparkle and the deep blue solemnity of the evening sky. Her eyes were a strange, dark, glittering grey, the colour of hematite, glowing as if from some implacable iron strength within. Her white arms peeked out from the billows of her hair; her left hand pressed against her hip and on her right was perched a beautiful mauve-pink bird. She held it out, shoulder high, but from time to time would bring it in close to her face and nuzzle its feathers with her splendid nose. Her legs, in sea-green trousers shot through with threads of gold, were crossed at the ankles, the right over the left, in a curiously jaunty pose, and she leaned back against the tower as if deliberately relaxing her regal bearing for Ruchel's sake, to lessen her awe. And, accordingly, a smile appeared on the crimson lips, gentle and beneficent, but revealing a set of such perfectly shaped, brilliant teeth that the effort to calm her onlooker was almost immediately undone.

For Ruchel was positively shaking now, from fear or excitement she couldn't have said. Shame was mixed up in it too, for in such company she couldn't help remembering how poor she was, how shabbily she was dressed. But somehow this creature didn't seem to mind, indeed was giving Ruchel her full attention, her manner suggesting that she was waiting for her to speak, to remark on her extraordinary personage perhaps, with a semblance of pluck or wit. But Ruchel, whose tongue could be so sharp that at times she blamed herself for losing a husband, was unable to utter a word. She forced herself to move the muscles of her mouth; and it would only make disgusting little circle-like shapes like the bubbling mouth of a fish, and her throat would eject no sound. Then the woman, kind and laughing, but nonetheless with impatience in her voice, which seemed to throb like a gong through the boulevards and avenues and piazzas, asked, 'Don't you recognise me, Ruchel? Don't you see who I am?'

Because of the clockface, Rachel thought of Keteb, then remembered the shadow. Then who? Lilith. Yes, it must be Lilith, the demon, the succubus, robber of infants and men's night fluids. Was this a test? Then how dismally she could fail. She longed to stay, but the teachings commanded her. She might have known: in her loneliness she had been wavering and all this was the test. She must flee this goldena medina, and keep its false, siren beauties safely out of her reach. She inwardly keened for Lev, for it was clear to her now as it had never been that he wasn't going to leave this place — no mortal man could resist. And she felt a sudden rush of irritation, no, anger, that men were such children, that the most pious and unworldly among them could let their heads be turned.

How long did this take, for Ruchel's emotions to transform themselves from wonder at this awesome lady to a rising scorn, and anger at all the gullible men in the world? A minute, maybe several, maybe only a split second. But it was all she needed to give her back her voice.

'I should have known,' said Ruchel. 'I'm not fooled.'

'Oh really?' the woman said, as though she was half-expecting this. 'But perhaps you are.'

Ruchel continued to look at her accusingly, but the woman shrugged. 'Oh, I know what you are thinking, Ruchel, and you are wrong. So very, very wrong. I know, you've been told that I am evil, a blasphemy — a witch or worse. This has been my special ignominy, an exquisite humiliation reserved for the likes of me. Do you realise how they slander me? Give me bad names, erase my true ones, to obscure my identity? To quiet me they have strapped me to their pedestals, or cast me down to the depths. And this has gone on for centuries! As long as I'm a goody-goody, like Ruth or Esther, I can't do any harm. Either that or I'm horny, spiteful Lilith, the devil. Either way I am kept in my place. And now even you are tricked into thinking that I am merely a demon, a goblin, a ghoul. Ach, I've come to expect it. Though, frankly, it has been mortifying — for someone like me.'

'That is pride.'

The woman gave Ruchel a sidelong glance. 'Ooh,' she said, 'how you speak to me, Ruchele! Still, it takes guts. I was beginning to think you had lost them. Maybe you are not the timid, whimpering soul I've taken you to be.'

'Only about some things,' Ruchel confessed.

'There is too much terror in you, Ruchele.'

Now Ruchel was sarcastic. 'Forgive me, it's been bred in my bones.'

The woman came closer, drawing away from the support of the tower. Its shadow clung to her, accenting the lustre of her skin, of the strange quicksilver eyes. 'I realise that, and it has saddened me. Don't you see? I am doing what I can to help. But you must trust me.'

She held out her hand, and with a flutter of its mauve-pink wings, the bird lifted off in a gliding, looping flight.

'Trust you?' Ruchel cried. 'This is the greatest blasphemy!'

At this the woman drew herself up to full height; with both hands free she pressed them to her hips and stood with her slippered feet firm on the ground and her legs wide apart. 'Oh come, Ruchel Kozminsky. I took you to be much cleverer than this. I thought that with you, for all your shortcomings, there was hope! How can you fill your head with such nonsense?'

'I am a simple woman,' Ruchel said.

'Yes, yes, indeed. Very simple. Tell me, who makes the money around your place? Puts the food on the table? Pays the taxes, cares for the children, applies the medicines, cleans the windowpanes, blacks the stove? In short, organises everything that needs to be done in that miserable household?'

'This is nothing.'

'Nothing. Nothing? Ruchele, it makes me weep to hear what you are saying. Although as you must understand, I am not the weeping kind.'

'No. Nor am I.'

'You see?'

Ruchel was beginning to. She sensed with a sudden prickling in her skin that she was being told things she had known and long forgotten. She nodded, as much to herself as to the imperious female who, with all the suppressed exasperation of a teacher, stood waiting before her. Finally Ruchel stilled herself, looked up and gave her a feeble smile.

'Well. That is more like it. This gives me heart. It seems I was not mistaken after all.'

'No, kayn aynhoreh, you were not.' Then, wishing to show herself capable of casting off old superstitions, Ruchel amended that. 'I mean to say, no, you were not.'

The woman sighed a sigh of great contentment and smiled. She stretched out her arm and, as if from nowhere, the beautiful bird glided towards her and skidded to a rest on her palm. It climbed onto her finger and the lady crossed her arms. For a time she did nothing more, content to observe her acolyte, her silvery gaze moving over her, measuring, assessing. Then she stroked the bird's feathers and tilted her head, indicating the gilded city, its glittering pyramids and tapered domes, the shiny fruit hanging from its trees, the streets paved with gold.

'Beautiful, isn't it?'

'Oh yes, yes it is,' Ruchel agreed.

'But quite strange, wouldn't you say?'

'I found it so, at first sight.'

'Do you know why?'

Ruchel, quite at ease now, permitted herself a laugh. 'Where I come from nothing looks like this.'

'Look again.'

Ruchel did as the lady asked, and saw this time an all too familiar sight: a landscape of muddy streets covered with ash, which floated in curled black flakes through the thinning tendrils of smoke, embers smouldering here and there, the charred, collapsed wall of the prayerhouse, or a store, and over everything a pall of silence. And it was only after she had stared at this scene for some time that Ruchel realised that the silence was the same as the silence of the golden city, for in neither were there any people — not a person, not a body, not a soul.

With her eyes wide with horror and wet with tears, Ruchel looked back at the lady.

'Go, Ruchele, go. For life. You will need all the courage I can give you, and America is no El Dorado, but go.'

———•———

There was an awful pain down one side of her neck, and when she lifted her hand to rub it she felt the muscles across her shoulder bunch up in a knot. She wriggled her shoulders and shook her aching arms. On the wooden table lay a perfectly round, springy mound of dough. Ruchel pressed a finger into it and was pleased to see the dent disappear almost as soon as it was made. Well, you know the rest: she put it aside to rise, took another mound that had already risen, swollen like a nursing breast to twice its size, plopped it into the greased pan, slipped it in the oven etc etc. All in the comforting, circling rhythm of her ritual. The sun came up, she was setting up her stall, she stared at the clock. Perhaps she expected to see someone there, partly obscured by its shadow. She shook her head, and laid out her wares. A fly came, but she hesitated before shooing it away. The hours passed. She gossiped with friends and the other stall-holders in the square as the sun traced an arc in the sky like the curve on her pumpernickel loaf.

And so it went, day by day, for a number of weeks until one day the word came from a neighbouring town that the tsar had issued another decree and that soldiers were hunting for Jewish boys to conscript them into the army, this time for an extra six years, on top of the standard twenty-five. Then Ruchel thought only of her son. She pulled out an old dress from her trunk, shook it and pressed it and thrust it onto Carl, who wriggled and swore and made faces in the darkening windowglass when she tried to fill out his hair with one of her wigs. Angry and frightened and tired, she told him to hush, yanking him by the upper arms and slapping a hollow between his shoulder blades to make him straighten up. And then she too saw the reflection in the glass, the ridiculous, ludicrous sight of him, and of her, yanking and slapping and shoving like some ill-bred peasant; and something snapped in her and tensed her jaw and she saw herself moving her head from side to side, slowly, deliberately — no. No. What was she afraid of? The boy was only seven! Yet her every action had been primed by fear. Ancient fear, crazing fear, over and over, fear. She turned to her mother and father who were already heading for bed, to lay cowering under the quilts, blinked, and snapped her head away. She ripped off the dress that hung in folds from Carl's shoulders and told him to put on his clothes. She rammed the dress into the trunk, pulled out a coat and a scarf, and a pair of Lev's old breeches, and threw these all on, stuffing her skirt into the legs of the pants as she hopped to a corner of the kitchen and reached deep into a bag of rye flour, extracting a coin sack and a bundle of notes. She took four of these notes, wetting her finger and counting them out, and placed them with great care under a glass on the table, reconsidered, took another from the bundle and left that, looked wildly about her and, remembering, broke off a bit of her yeast and wrapped it in a cloth, grabbed a valise and some bread, her three little daughters and her son, and that very night left the village, following the route that Lev had taken the four different times she had refused to go with him.

They rode in a cart to the nearest town, the children asleep in the straw and the stars so close they seemed to prickle the back of her neck. There was a succession of carts, lumbering and stumbling, and train carriages after that, and one night spent in a field of tall grass where they hid when they heard the carousing Cossacks trotting past, until they got to a river and Ruchel bribed her way onto a barge; then walking as far as the next train, moving when they could at night, and then at last the blustery port of Danzig and the hold of the cattle ship over rocking northern seas and the five of them arriving hungry but healthy, gott zu danken and thanks too to the Ellis Island officials, in America; New York.

Heroic? Ruchel thought so, though at times their progress had seemed as plodding and as measured as an ant's over a patch of dirt. Or as slow as scraps skimming a silty puddle in the old market square. Now, of course, we have the language for this: it's relativity, we would say, but even though she hadn't the words for it, I have a feeling in my bones that Ruchel thought of it first. But the point is that when she wasn't thinking she was moving, and every bridge she crossed, every field and sea, made her feel marvellously, exuberantly, thankfully alive.

She stood with her four children at the iron gates of the city and was filled with such wonder at the ships and the crowds and the tall buildings on the other side of the bay swamped in a sooty, golden haze that she announced to Lev's brother Meyer, who'd been waiting for them in that swarm of people, that they weren't in a hurry yet to hop on the train out west. 'Meyer, I want to see a real city — just once.' So they took a spanking new ferry across the mouth of the Hudson to Manhattan and they saw the streets of people and the peddlers and their barrows and ate ice-cream in biscuity cones. They had fun, oh how they had fun, though Ruchel could see that here too in America the people were poor; but she tried for the moment not to think of that. The most exciting thing of all was to climb on an omnibus, a double-decker one — you know, the small kind pulled by horse — and they sat in the open air at the top, far above the pungent fumes of the city, and rode on the avenues past the fine granite mansions uptown; and Ruchel took off Lev's scarf and let her hair that had grown inch by inch throughout the long journey float free and, as the bus lurched and swayed to a halt in some snarl of carriages and horses, she caught a reflection in the shimmering glass of one of a series of tall, ornamental windows on a mock baroque facade. It was that of a woman, an astonishingly beautiful woman, with flaming hair covering her shoulders in a tumult of waves and curls.

A Proposed Marriage

Suzanne Edgar

Swami wheeled his barrow past the sign 'Vasua Reef Resort welcomes you!' and went around the building to the kitchen where he knocked, certain that here at least he would be successful.

Thelua poked his head out.

'What you want?'

Curried fish and coconut steamed out with him, making Swami's stomach jump.

'I am bringing the veg. Tomato, cucumber, coriander —'

'Tole you. Not so many tourists since the coup.'

Swami folded back the tarpaulin so that his green and red vegetables glistened in the morning sun.

'You hear me?' Thelua shouted.

'But —'

The door was slammed.

Marching forward Swami saluted that old brown door with the paint peeling. He felt like kicking it. 'Yes sir!' He had to replace the tarpaulin watched by the grinning yard sweeper; the swish of his broom conveyed an infuriating pity. Swami spat. As he hoisted the barrow with its useless load and pushed it away, he sensed the fellow's eye on him and his back curled.

When he finished in the fields that evening he changed and walked back to the resort. In the cool, dim Paradise Bar he watched bubbles dissolving on the surface of his beer. A girl with golden knees perched on the stool next to him and tapped her long, polished nails on the counter.

'Great band!' she said.

'You are staying here?'

'Till tomorrow.'

He wished he had the money to buy her a drink.

'Like to dance?' he asked, climbing off his stool.

The girl, Patty, held herself so close to him on the dance floor that sweat broke out on the palms of his hands. They slid down her thin dress to rest on her bottom.

'Off you go, Naidu. Not allowed here in thongs.' A heavy hand dropped on his shoulder.

'Excuse me, Madam.' Patty's hands were prised off Swami's shoulder blades and he let himself be pushed away.

As he walked up the track home the sense of her knees nudging his as they danced stayed with him. He could have made it with that girl.

The family were eating while his father read out bits from the *Fiji Times*: another Indian shopkeeper had been stabbed in Suva.

'At least it is quiet out here,' his mother said, her eyes darting from one face to another.

His father brushed away this foolishness with an impatient hand. 'Only a matter of time.'

'We should leave Fiji.' Swami jerked his chin up and met their stares.

'Little brother has big ideas, eh?' Raman snickered. 'Very smart. Very naive actually.'

Their mother noticed her daughter-in-law's face.

'Shanti, bring more rice.'

Shanti's family lived in Suva. She rushed from the table and banged the door behind her as she left the room. Swami listened. He could not hear her moving around the kitchen but it was a long time before she came back with the rice.

In the morning he heard her weeping through the partition, in the other part of the room that she and Raman shared with their sons. 'The children,' she kept moaning.

Raman growled. 'Fijians take over business? Sit around drinking kava all day . . .'

Swami closed his eyes and a vision came to him: he would find a foreign wife, someone like Patty. Once settled with her in Australia he could bring out the others. He pictured a vast silvery bridge stretching across the waves from Sydney to Nadi. At one end he stood, welcoming arms held forward; at the other were his parents, his brothers and sisters and their children. Carrying suitcases and coloured plastic bags, they stepped gaily onto their end of the bridge. He felt his heart swell with tenderness and heroism.

For months there had been little rain, but he hardly noticed the earth's hardness that morning, for as he dug he thought about his plan and worked on the details. He would use a new name, no Australian girl could be expected to cope with Munswami Hari Naidu. He'd be Roddy, Rod as they became intimate; again he saw Patty's sun-ripened knees. To find another young lady he would simply avoid the bars and take the track through the river to the resort beach. They always lay about there on lounges, worshipping the sun. His mother often told him he was handsome, his skin was lighter than his brothers' and his body still slim and straight. She held high hopes for him — at last he saw a path to this future.

He told his father that he was going to look for new outlets for their vegetables, and propping his hoe against the mango tree, hurried to the river where he washed the dust from his body and combed his hair. On a curve of sand between lagoon and hotel the beach beauties lay. He stepped forward. But it was rather exposed and he edged back into the shelter of the bush before trying a more secluded spot further down. A lady was swaying on a hammock, little cushions of her white flesh squeezed through the corded diamonds of the rope. The trees' shadows fingered her and on the ground beneath the hammock a pair of sunglasses encrusted with diamantes glittered.

He glided to her side. 'Good morning.'

'Are you staff?' She lowered her magazine. 'Nothing, thank you.' Ice-blue eyes peered at Swami above the magazine that she was now using for a fan.

'Very fine weather we are having? Very dry and sunny.'

'You'd better be on your way or I'll call someone.' She wobbled over the side of the hammock and onto her feet. Purple veins ran up her legs.

Swami melted into the shadows again.

The next morning he had a good idea and picked some bananas before changing into his best shirt to visit

Vasua. Two young girls about his age sat on the sand under the coconut palms. Near the hotel an Indian gardener slowly moved his hose from one bright lily to another, and out in the lagoon Fijians were dragging a net for fish. He positioned himself so close to the girls that he could smell the perfumed oil they were rubbing on each other's backs.

'Do you mind if I accompany your sunbake?' He settled onto his haunches.

'Okay by me,' the blonde one said. 'Okay with you, Ros?'

Her girlfriend giggled. There were freckles on her face, but in the green bikini her body was white as coconut cream.

'You staying here at Ritzville?' she smiled.

'I own a rice plantation over in the valley.' Swami pointed, 'People work it for me.'

'You must be *rich*.' She rolled over and sat up to inspect him.

Swami lowered his eyes modestly and removed the bananas from inside his shirt. Just as he was about to offer them, he heard whistles from the lagoon. Two youths ran up the beach, pulling off snorkels and masks and shouting at the girls to bring their towels.

Ros and the blonde jumped up and Ros shrugged.

'Sorry. We're slaves, y'see. Have to obey orders.' Her friend was mincing down the beach and she followed her. 'See ya!'

He knew that he only needed to improve his technique, so he haunted the beach. When he came home repeatedly with no new buyers for their vegetables, his father called him good-for-nothing and refused to let him off work. Swami's tongue was tied; he felt he could not reveal the plan to the family until he had something definite to announce, news of an engagement.

On Sunday he was dozing on the step, only half seeing the parched fields where spindles of sugar cane waved forlornly. He started up every few minutes to slap the bored flies ambling up and down his legs. Then, suddenly, the afternoon jerked awake to the rumble of Satendra's truck labouring up the track.

'Coming to Sigatoka?' his friend bellowed above the roar of the engine that he always left running in case of starting troubles. Satendra's wife and little girl were in the cabin so Swami climbed onto the tray behind.

In town when they'd finished shopping, they met for a cup of tea at Lim's Cafe. Swami leaned back and stretched his arm along the top of the alcove.

'I have been thinking of getting married,' he announced.

Satendra paused in the act of placing a cake in his mouth.

'I thought you were opposed to early marriage!'

'Your mother is arranging something?' his wife said.

'Actually I prefer a more modern approach.'

Even little Malini was watching him. Swami took another slow sip of tea, enjoying their suspense.

'One of the girls from school, is it?' Satendra was leaning forward now.

'I will not be taking an Indian wife.'

Satendra's wife dropped her eyes.

'I shall be marrying an Australian.'

They all clamoured at once. 'Tell us, man!'

He quietened them with one wave of his hand and refused to say more. They could infer whatever they liked, he let his manner suggest; he insisted on paying for their tea and cakes.

Satendra's wife put a hand on her husband's arm. 'Let him,' she said. 'It's a celebration we are having.'

Sweeping crumbs from the table, Swami called the waiter.

On the way home Swami saw ripe coconuts growing in the bush and he signalled Satendra to stop. 'For Malini!' he shouted and ran across the road and up the tree's sloping trunk. He was handing the coconut through the truck's window when a tourist van screeched to a halt on the other side of the road.

'What you doing?' the driver bawled.

Swami flicked his eyes up and down the road: there was no-one in sight but himself and his friends. In the van four white faces were pressed to the windows.

'Nothing.'

The driver was a big Fijian, one elbow hung over the window edge. 'Thieving government property.'

'For the child,' Swami stammered.

The receiver of stolen goods hung her head.

The driver opened his door and stepped down heavily to the road. 'Thieving Indian beggar,' he said distinctly. 'Put it back.'

Swami flipped the coconut into the grass. The driver watched, hands on hips, then turned and threw a laughing comment to his passengers.

'Let's go,' Swami muttered to Satendra and heaved himself over the side of the truck.

Satendra stalled the engine. The tourists kept on gaping. After three tries, it sputtered into life and they made their get-away.

———•———

It was dusk and Swami was walking home from the cowshed when he saw the figure of a woman in pink drifting along the track near their farm. His chest tightened as she stopped to speak; golden curls shimmered round her head.

'Am I trespassing? Is this your property?' Her words had a lilt and their politeness made him drop the hoe.

'Most welcome. Perhaps I can accompany you? Track is getting very rough once you cross the stream.' She was wearing flimsy gold sandals. 'Will be very dark soon, actually.'

'Why not?'

He fell in beside her, not daring to look at her face but aware of a perfume, bangles tinkling and the skirt swinging from wide hips to brush her calves. If he drew himself up, he was just taller than she.

'I am Munswami Naidu,' he said. 'Actually, people call me Roddy.'

'Alanna,' she smiled and stretched out a hand. 'I'm from Sydney. I'd rather call you Mun . . .'

'Swami. Munswami.'

She fluttered her white hands and the bangles jingled. 'I'd better stick to Roddy.'

What was she doing, wandering up their rutted track at this time of day in such fancy clothes? She seemed heaven-sent.

'How lucky you are to live in this peaceful valley. I came to see the rice, I've never seen it growing. But there doesn't appear to be any?' She blinked at the stubbled fields.

'We harvested in early May.

Alanna stumbled over a pebble and bent to adjust her sandal.

'That's my father on our tractor,' Swami pointed. 'It's new. We bought it last year.'

But Alanna spread both arms wide as if embracing the round hills, the fields and their two cows; she let out a long sigh as a full moon slid through the green sky.

The Fijian boys who helped Mr Chan went past in dirty shorts, one of them riding his white horse.

'Such a *sensual* landscape,' she breathed. 'Very Gauguin.'

He asked her about Australia, but she kept talking about the healer she'd visited in Vutua; Alanna had slept for two hours when she got back to the resort, she felt so purified. 'A freeing. You know? Great karma. Such *tension* in Sydney.'

'Here, too.'

'Since the coup you mean?'

He nodded and told her about the troubles, although she knew a lot already. They turned back when the forest began, and as they passed the farmhouse, Swami said, 'I shall go with you to the highway?'

They strolled along till they came to the road and the corrugated iron stall where the Naidus used to sell their vegetables. He had painted a sign: 'Veg, Fruits, World Leader'.

'Would you like to come over to Vasua for a drink?' she said.

'Actually it is not allowed to visit there in flip-flops.'

'You'd be *my* guest.'

He took her elbow to guide her across the Queen's Road. 'I'll show you a short cut through the river. It is shallow because of the drought.'

She followed him trustfully into the bush and as they passed the workers' bures, children playing in the light from the doorways looked up to admire his new friend.

When the brightness beaming like a searchlight from

the resort hit them, Swami saw Alanna's face. Her cheeks were lined and a scrawny neck betrayed her. Even the cloud of fair hair showed grey roots. Cosmetics lent a false rosiness to her cheeks, a smudge to the rims of her eyes. His stomach dropped with such a thud that he paused. She must be nearly thirty years older than him. Still, such women could be lonely, that was why they travelled, they would be very devoted . . .

She turned and waited for him to catch up, smiling expectantly, and he readjusted his face.

'We'll see if Paul's awake, my husband,' she said. 'He'd like to meet you. He's following the politics.'

It was the last straw. What a hoax. He stared at a red-throated hibiscus shrilling what he should have realised.

'I don't feel welcome in this part of the resort,' he hung back. 'I'll get bad looks from the bar boys.'

'You're with *me*,' Alanna said. 'You're my *friend*.' She led the way, beckoning. Her arms were sinewy too, how could he have been such an idiot?

When her back was turned he combed his hair and tucked in his shirt. At least he'd get a beer off them. Damn-fool tourists, more money than sense. She took him up the back stairs to collect her husband from their suite and they all walked down the corridor to the Paradise Bar. While Alanna's husband bought drinks, she led Swami out to the wicker chairs around tables on the terrace. He had never sat on the terrace before.

Although Paul Hughes was a greybeard, you could see he was wondering what on earth his wife had picked up. Swami shifted his chair away from Alanna's; as if he'd make a move on a woman her age! He drummed his fingers on the table. Let her start the conversation, she'd cooked up this scene.

As Alanna drank her tequila sunrise, the cherry on the side of her glass glowed. The moon swung under the coconut palms and dance music wafted from the Honeymooners' Restaurant. Swami smelt the food the rich ate.

'We've been watching your politics,' Paul said. 'I don't like the look of this Taukei mob.'

'Thugs.' Swami drained his glass. The beer loosened his tongue and he started telling them a few facts.

Paul turned his chair so that he was facing Swami. 'Where were *you* when you heard about the coup?'

'Lunchtime we rest under the mango tree. Shanti came running with our food. "Government have been arrested by the army!" she said. She brought the radio. I said, "The Queen will not allow." But my father knew. "Indian people are finished in Fiji," he said.'

Their kindly faces had led Swami to say more than he'd meant; he looked out to where the sea tossed froth over the reef with a hushing sound.

'You're scapegoats,' Alanna said. 'The Nazis went in for that sort of thing.'

Paul turned round to her and his face lit up. 'Roddy sounds like us talking about our coup —'

But she waved her tinkling wrists indignantly. 'Come on! Ours wasn't *violent*.'

He wished they'd offer him another beer.

'We built this country,' he said. 'From nothing.'

'Of course, it's early days yet,' Paul coughed.

Swami wasn't letting them off that easily. 'Actually people are thrown in gaol without trial. A priest even. For letting Mr Nandan pray in the temple,' he said loudly.

Alanna's eyes widened. 'What can you do?'

He noticed his feet, in the thongs, and tucked them

under the chair. He decided not to tell them about the incident with the coconut but he longed to plead, 'Take me back to Sydney with you.'

'People want to get away,' he said. His hands were shaking and the beer mug slipped from his fingers and fell with a clunk on the glass-topped table.

Alanna reached over and patted his arm. He snatched it back, but saw that she'd only meant to comfort him and he felt sorry when a flush crept up her neck.

Paul heaved his bony frame out of the chair. 'I'll get another round. Same again?'

It was hopeless, with the second beer Swami felt even more emotional. He stood up. 'I must go.'

'It's been a privilege,' Paul stood too and extended his thin hand.

'Lovely talking with you, Rod,' Alanna's bracelets rang and shone in the moonlight.

'You would like to come to our home for dinner? My mother would be honoured.'

They exchanged a married look and Paul straightened his tie. 'Afraid we're committed, friends. Our last night, you know.'

Alanna would not meet Swami's eye.

He bowed.

'Goodbye. Thank you very much.' Thrusting a piece of paper with his name and address on it into Alanna's hand, he hurried through the darkness at the edge of the glittering terrace.

Squelching along the damp sand, he kicked a clam shell in front of him. How stupid his plan had been. These Australian women were so bossy, who'd want one for a wife? He glanced back at the hotel where explosions of song and laughter were bursting like fireworks from the yellow windows. She and the husband would be in there, dancing, stuffing themselves with food.

The moon shone for a moment on the pale eyes of a dead fish stranded by the tide. He picked it up and sprinted over the sand to where a tree was silhouetted against the sky. Tearing off a leaf, he wrapped up the fish before heading for their rooms in the eastern wing of the hotel. With the parcel inside his shirt, he shinned up the verandah pole to the balcony. They had gone out leaving only the screen door shut. Softly, he eased it back and moved inside.

From the bathroom door a shaft of light fell across the room and onto a red suitcase. He hovered. The bed, the wardrobe? They were leaving tomorrow . . . Little heaps of discarded clothes lay here and there about the floor. Treading carefully between them, he tiptoed to the suitcase and raised the lid, releasing a scent of roses. Inside were carefully packed layers of slithery dresses. He raised one and folded his parcel underneath.

Then he crept out, slid down the pole and running lightly, made for home. Only when he gained the hard asphalt surface of the road did his hatred subside and a feeling of triumph lift his spirits.

At the River

LIBBY HATHORN

Sometimes Johnny felt the growth, the heat and the growth of the place would be what annihilated him here. Or that he'd just grow into the jungle like those ugly taut vines strangling trees every which way. Vines that could look like veins running the pale inside of Tesoriro's arms when he worked out early mornings, pumped up and lethal. Then he'd be utterly oppressed by the indolent talk of his companions. The indolent talk and the heat and the growth and the waiting would seem inescapable, endless.

He'd been forced to know things too intimately up here in this strange hot jungle country, places, and parts of bodies, a new working vocabulary to describe them. The hot damp foreignness was now just part of a frightening yet familiar routine of death and life, the grind of a war.

Today he had to get away from the base. And not to the 'suck fuck' parlours in the nearest town where the others were heading and where Tesoriro would insist noisily he should go. There were tracks that fanned out from the base, any number of them leading down to the river. He chose the usual one that led to a large clearing and the relief to be had looking out onto the stretch of green water, all alone.

'Don't be like that bloody minister's son,' Tesoriro had told him often enough when he saw Johnny heading off again. 'Poor bastard never did anything but sit on his bed reading his Bible. And then one day, quiet as any-thing, went off to the river, mate, and blew his bloody brains out. Don't be like Matthews. Come on with us. Your girlfriend'll keep mate.'

'My wife,' Johnny would say, knowing it annoyed, maybe even puzzled Tesoriro, the hours he spent writing to Frannie.

'Same diff,' he'd say, 'she's there and you're here. So c'mon why don't ya?' But today Tesoriro didn't insist, perhaps reading Johnny's mood.

Johnny hadn't liked Arnold Tesoriro at first, found him too intrusive altogether. He was loud-mouthed and known even in this company to be hot-headed. 'Don't want bloody Tessy with us,' the tankies would joke, 'if we want to bloody come back alive!' But they sought his company because he made them laugh. And Johnny liked him in the end because he was generous to everyone, even the knots of kids always hanging around who'd come to pinch things from the base.

In some ways it seemed to Johnny that Arnold Tesoriro was a bit of a kid himself. But a kid suffering something all right when the laughing and the fooling around finally stopped. Sometimes late at night after a lot of bacardi, Arnold would get serious, talk about things, home, a lot about home. And eventually he'd come round to it.

'Shit man the fucking guilt. Hadn't known this kind of thing since high school when I dobbed somebody in for a crime I'd committed. And then heard the poor bastard caned. But this — it gets to you. Jesus! Guilt for coming here in the first place. For bloody surviving when your mates don't.

'And when you go on leave mate, well that's another kind. That's a beauty! See in my hometown this woman I knew — a teacher, I really liked her too — well when she saw me coming down the main street my first leave, she spat at me. How'd you like that? You grow up in a town and you think you know people and they know you and then — spat at by somebody you like right on the main street. God! And knowing plenty of others'd like to. Holy shit, that's another kind of guilt being on leave, the worst!'

Arnold Tesoriro needed people round him all the time. It was his way of coping with things here. He couldn't quite understand that Johnny needed to be solitary for the same reason. A long time ago, just a few weeks after his arrival in Vietnam, Johnny had realised it was going to be hard to hold on through the long grim months. He'd practised a switch-off mechanism that had helped him as a small boy get through the difficult first months of separation from his mother. Admittedly it was more difficult here with constant and bloody reminders that he was in the middle of a war he soon realised was going to be impossible to win. This war was unlike the others he knew so much about from his grandfather who'd seen two of them. This war, with no beachhead to storm, no front and no rear, just these seemingly endless months of skirmishes, boredom and fear, was different to what he'd expected all right.

Arnold Tesoriro didn't seem to have any fear, something Johnny found strange, but he had a lot of anger. He'd told Johnny the first night he'd moved into his tent that he'd come up here for the usual reasons. 'To contain communism, what do you bloody think? To support the American alliance, I believed in that! To have fun! Maybe, though I really came up here to nick supplies for the gooks and the nuns?' And he'd laughed that loud grating laugh.

On the path to the river now Johnny was annoyed to find a villager — a woman bringing a small child with her. She bowed her head so it was difficult to see her face. But the child smiled at him. The woman pulled the baby tight to her side. When she did look up her eyes, bright with fear, seemed young but there were deep circles under them, and lines on her face; she was not as young as he'd first thought.

'It's okay,' he said wearily, noticing the bright pink cake of soap clasped like a treasure in her hand and realising she was going down to bathe as some of the villagers did here. 'It's okay,' and he turned back to find another path. He went in among the canes a little further on, plunging downwards to another less accessible place. But though it was downstream from the woman and her child it was not sufficiently far. At first he was annoyed to hear her soft, coaxing voice and the splashing of water. But then there were cries of pleasure from the child, a good sound, he thought tiredly as he lit a cigarette . . .

For a moment he could clearly remember other such cries in the surf back home. That great wash of shrieks and falling water and the fantastical rhythm of a summer's day. Maroubra Beach with Frannie in those first weeks of their knowing each other. He was glad he could still hang on to the thought of her and the way it had been in that place — not a dream place, though it might as well be. God the simplicity of everything then. It made him feel old just thinking about it, thinking about her! There would never be summer days like those again because when he went back there'd be no way of letting all this go. The immense and steadily growing weight of it. He'd be flawed forever by this fucking place, he knew it.

Tesoriro might think he'd come here this afternoon to write to Frannie but he hadn't written to her in days, no, not in weeks. He felt empty and exhausted as if he had nothing he could tell her about this place that was robbing him even of words. Some part of him was being put on hold in an endless glaring summer, filled from time to time with sudden blasts of sound like a roaring Sydney surf, and those human cries that were not joyous.

As he squatted there in the dappled glade a large spider descended and bit his hand, where it rested on the cane. He checked, not poisonous, although the bloody thing looked big enough to be. He shook it away. It slithered down his leg and hit the ground where he stamped the life out of it. He stared at the crushed body not wanting to, but remembering the burial he'd witnessed on patrol last week. He'd seen Andy and Dennis jump on 'the bloody nogs,' dead VC soldiers stiff as boards. They'd jumped on them to break their backs so that they'd fit more easily into the compact shallow graves they'd prepared. What disturbed him was that at the time it hadn't seemed a particularly dreadful thing to do. After the shock of the first few months here he was aware of a diminution of response that was frightening. If he stayed here much longer a kind of monster might go back home with just the outer shell of that supposedly decent young man who'd gone away to fight for his country.

The splashing, less vigorous now, and the creaking of bamboo, were the only sounds. If he parted the canes, he thought idly, he might very well see the woman and child in the river, and he moved forwards for that view. She was in the water, her bare back exposed as she soaped the child's body. She was making soft sensuous sounds as she splashed water over the child's foaming shoulders and head before swirling her round in the green river. He could see the exact curve of the woman's spine as she bent forward. Then, suddenly, in a slow deliberate movement, she stood up throwing back her head to release her hair. The silky cascade came tumbling down. It was breathtaking, the beauty of the uncoiling hair slithering down that tender back. (He was startled by it, by what it caused him to feel.) She turned suddenly towards him for a moment, to place the washed child on the bank.

Now he watched intently as she faced the child and made vigorous movements with the soap over her own thin body. First along one arm then along the other, then over her breasts and stomach, between her legs and down each one, lifting them in turn, like a dancer, from the water so that even her feet, her toes, did not escape this loving attention. Her lustrous hair swung around her shoulders, slithered over her wet back and clung there until she tossed her head again and the curtain of it flew out and up and around. He was fascinated, could not take his eyes off the swinging hair and the busy arms of the woman washing. He felt a tenderness towards her stirring, something he'd never felt about any of the women up here, something that made him feel weak and sorry and glad. In observing the ordinariness of her actions, the scrupulous washing of the child and her own dainty ritual in the river, he was seeing a woman. Not a young woman or even a beautiful woman, though there was a beauty he recognised. A woman. Just that. He didn't want her to leave.

But she did, stepping up the bank gracefully and moving out of sight with the baby girl. He allowed the canes to snap back into position and sat alone for some time, feeling the pain of the spider bite now. Someone had stashed some bacardi and he would probably drink a lot tonight, he thought. At least he'd be alone until late.

But on the path quite near the camp a child stepped out of the shadows. He recognised the boy, maybe nine or ten years old, the pinched face of hunger that was nevertheless well versed in the language of smiles — the new kid and the one Arnold said was different from the others who hung around. This one Arnold had singled out for special treatment, extra provisions. He hadn't asked why, knowing Arnold did this sort of thing for reasons of his own.

'Sick,' the boy said urgently with no smiles tonight. 'Very sick. Mother. Please.'

'Bugger Tesoriro,' he thought, 'encouraging this kid the way he did.'

'Arnold's not here. Gone off into town, okay? Back very late, okay? Now bugger off.'

'You to come,' the child insisted and Johnny felt a surge of anger.

'Not me mate,' he answered. He wouldn't be chosen.

'Get involved and you're dead,' he'd thought after Arnold had taken him to the orphanage where he kept some nuns in stolen medical supplies. After what he'd seen Johnny didn't want to go there again. Arnold's different, he told himself on the silent ride back to base. It makes him feel good to get involved like this.

'Sick, please come.' He shrugged the boy off and went into the tent, though not before giving him a tin of something. But the boy sat outside in the dark. Johnny sprawled on the camp stretcher. Staring out, into a more than usual darkness and he sensed the boy's anxious presence nearby. He closed his eyes. The child finally took courage, parting the tent flap and treading so softly across the duckboard flooring that Johnny didn't hear him until he touched his arm. He jumped up and swore.

'You come?' he asked as if he knew that in the end Johnny would give in. In the end he did, going angrily down the familiar path to the edge of the village. All the way there the child chanted, thank you, thank you, deliberately and clearly in a flat, unemotional voice.

He found the mother in a tiny hut set apart from the others, alone on a bed of rags, sick with fever and burns. He left aspirins, all he had till Tesoriro got back, and he promised he'd try to bring a doctor the next morning. He had to get out of there before anything happened. She was going to die soon you could see it at a glance — he couldn't take such close contact. But the boy delayed him, 'Thank you,' he said over and over now in a tone of gratitude and handling the foiled packet of tablets with a sickening reverence. Johnny went stumbling back to base again, not angry but resentful he'd been accorded such magic by the boy in Tesoriro's absence.

He drank a lot of bacardi but didn't seem to get drunk. So he sat sombrely, looking out onto other tents, packed with their sandbags and corrugated iron, thinking of the boy in the dark whose mother would die by morning. He felt a surge of pity for both of them, more for the boy. He lay down finally but couldn't sleep at first as he waited for the sound of the motors along the jungle road and Tesoriro who could take over the problem. He dozed a little, saw in the swaying shadows outside images of the woman in the river with the cascade of loose hair. The river. He sat up sweaty, uneasy.

Sometime after midnight he remembered something. The medical supply. The morphine and the other stronger pain killers in row after row of white packets. And he thought he might break in the way Tesoriro had shown him and take some stronger stuff to the woman. It would make it easier on the boy.

The track back to the hut was filled with looming shadows this time. But an anger for the boy keeping vigil, who tonight seemed so like he had been all those years back, drove him on. Sitting by his own bed afraid to get into cold sheets, afraid to sleep, afraid to think of the loss and what it might mean — the night Johnny's mother had finally left their house. He would give the sick woman the stolen drugs then he'd go across to the fucking village and get someone to help the boy, that's what he'd do! Why were the villagers ignoring this little kid anyway? Why was a child as young as he left to cope with a death alone?

Tesoriro came in noisy and drunk, but not so drunk he couldn't listen to Johnny's story.

'You went alone to the village in the middle of the night? Jesus!'

'I only managed to get a half mad mama san in the end. No-one else would come out.'

'I don't bloody wonder,' Tesoriro said.

'Look mate, that kid's an outcast. Haven't you noticed? The other kids ignore him most of the time. I don't know the full story but his mother did something the rest of the villagers don't like. With the VC I guess. And they're punishing her deadset. Leaving her to die by inches. And punishing the kid.'

'But if one of the older women from the village actually went with you — I s'pose that's a good sign.' Tesoriro sank onto his bed yawning. 'I'll go over in the morning, first thing,' he muttered before closing his eyes.

Johnny lay on his bed. He thought maybe he would write to Frannie tomorrow and tell her all about the boy and his mother. Yes! He'd tell her about the other woman with the kid at the river, too. The way she'd played with the child, and how he'd been touched by it in a way that the kids in the orphanage had somehow not been able to touch him, or the stiff as board soldiers unceremoniously despatched had not. And how it was possible that a foreign woman bathing in a river could remind him so much of home, and of her.

As good as his word Tesoriro checked the hut at the edge of the village next morning.

'Gone,' he announced flatly when he arrived back in the steamy first light. His face was harsh. 'Decamped. God knows where. Both of them.'

'She couldn't have moved by herself,' Johnny began, 'she was . . .' Tesoriro was lying, trying to save him from the piece of news he already knew.

'Both of them?' he asked bitterly. 'The kid too?'

Tesoriro nodded.

'You did good, mate,' Tesoriro began, 'you did what you thought was best. It's not your bloody fault. Don't go thinking that for Christ sake.'

Later he heard Tesoriro singing soldier songs, and he knew it was for his sake.

Johnny began writing the letter to Frannie that morning but he didn't have time to finish it. They were to be on the move later in the day. When he returned from this next operation at Long Tan he'd finish it. He'd tell Frannie everything. How he'd changed. How Tesoriro had helped change him. How he hadn't grown up, not really, not until he'd got here. And how he wanted them to have a child as soon as he got back and forget the five-year delay they'd planned. Even the house they'd wanted to buy with the war service loan he'd get, part of the reason he'd come up here in the first place. Part of the plan he had for them. Forget bloody plans altogether.

He put the several closely written pages out of Tesoriro's sight; he was always so curious. But it would be Tesoriro who would doggedly go searching to find the secret pages and send them on home to Australia and to Frannie.

Be Prepared

DOROTHY JOHNSTON

'It's the dog days.'

Willy's mother says this when he asks her to take him to Dickson pool. Then she says, 'No, what is he thinking of?'

It's perfectly clear to Willy what he's thinking of, but he's scared to repeat it. He makes a noise in his throat and says in his helpful voice, 'When Emily wakes up?'

His mother says she'll be glad when he's back at school.

Willy badly wants to point out that he could go on his own, wheel his bike across Northbourne Avenue, not ride it; and he won't drown. He chews the inside of his mouth, knowing that whatever he says now will only make his mother crosser.

A little later he tells her, 'I'm going for a ride. Don't worry, I won't go off the bike path.'

He takes his time getting his bike out of the shed, shaking a rag and wiping the paint where it's dusty from yesterday's ride. It's the kind of summer where dust gathers quickly in any place. His wheels scurf up dust where you'd least expect it. When he's out riding, he watches it fluff under cars. It rises from the ground as if grateful for any change, or chance at all. He wipes his blue and silver paintwork, dawdling.

He used to feel a dag wearing his stackhat, only now he doesn't think about it. His head felt queer and naked once when he forgot, as though someone had shaved all his hair off. He has no particular destination in mind; he's ridden through these summer holidays in circles. There's nowhere he can possibly think of that he hasn't already been. Each destination occupies a distinct physical space in his mind, and he can study it the way he might study places on a map, or a grid plan of the city.

Last year his teacher taught them about town planning; one week for a project they had to draw their own. Willy could think of nothing until the night before his project had to be handed in, and then he drew a plan for a city where people got around entirely by bicycle, where bikes were welcome everywhere. This plan, which his teacher said was 'Interesting, Wilfred, but a little impractical?' springs into Willy's head from time to time; he wishes Canberra was more like that.

They lie there, on the surface of his mind, the places he has been and could go, different parts of his suburb and the next — is allowed to go — for although he does not often break his word to his mother, sometimes he veers off the bike path. He is not afraid of her finding out — how can she, unless he tells her? After Emily wakes up, the furthest she'll go, if she goes anywhere, will be the O'Connor shops. His afternoon rides are for his mother's benefit, so she can have the house to herself while Emily's asleep.

She asks him questions in the mornings. She asks, 'Why don't you go over to Alex's?', so that he has to remind her that Alex is away.

'What about Robert?'

'He's away too!'

It hurts to repeat these tuneless facts. He wouldn't mind so much that his two best friends are away if his mother didn't keep on forgetting.

At the playground off Condamine Street he'll see the same kids who tease him, and who won't share their fruit boxes. He wishes some interesting unknown place would just spring up. He looks to the right and the left, but there's only the same gum trees drawn into themselves, leaves turned side on to the sun; and the dead grass like hairs on an old balding man, and the dust rising, underneath. He knows what a mirage is, and hopes for one of these too, a place which does not exist but draws him towards it through the heat. A mystery to solve would be best.

The summer did have a high point — one Friday afternoon when his father came home early from work, and they took a picnic tea to the Cotter. The air was still and clear, and there were long shadows across the sand. Picnicking families were scattered about, and groups of people swam and splashed in the water. Half-a-dozen kids were throwing a large coloured ball, which cracked like a gun shot every time it hit the water, and the casuarinas took up the sound and passed it down the river.

Willy helped his mother take off all of Emily's clothes and they held her between them in the warm shallow water. Emily grabbed a handful of sand and was going to eat it, but Willy gently took it from her. She grinned and giggled, and splashed with both hands, and he splashed her back.

'Will!' his father called, from out in the water. 'Swim to me!' And he did! That's what the whole evening was like, until it got too dark to see. His father and mother and sister and him, all connected by the water, like four points on a rectangle.

Willy hoped that next Friday they could go again. He offered to prepare the picnic food all by himself. But his parents were invited somewhere — some grown-ups only affair. He had to stay behind with Emily and the babysitter.

———•———

'What is your name?'

'Willy.' He shades his eyes to look at the man. The sun makes both their faces flat.

'For Will—iam?' The man laughs, a high soft sound, as though he's pleased with himself. He steps back on one foot, with both hands on his hips.

'Wilfred — but no-one ever calls me that.'

The man laughs again, and nods. 'Okay.' When he laughs, his eyes go more squinty than ever.

'What's your name?'

'Tan. My name is Tan.'

'This's my cub hall,' Willy says. 'What're you doing here?'

'I live here.'

'*Live* here? How come?'

Tan looks embarrassed, then says sharply, 'Badger — you know Badger?'

Of course Willy knows Badger.

'Badger, he have ask me to stay — to be — how is it called? Caretaker. Hey — would you like drink — cool drink?'

Willy grins. 'Sure, dude!' He wheels his bike across to the wall and starts fiddling with the chain. He feels a bit funny about going inside, but after all, it *is* his cub hall.

Tan pushes the heavy door so that it opens wide, and Willy follows him. Inside, it's cool and dim. Willy smells the dust rising from the wooden floor, and blinks to get his bearings. Tan goes straight to the kitchen, takes a jug of orange cordial from the fridge and pours them both a glass. Willy drinks his without stopping, and wipes his mouth with the back of his hand. He stares around at the familiar objects on the walls; the scarves, pinned, overlapping, their different colours denoting different cub and scout packs, the portraits of the Queen and Baden Powell, the flags and wooden plaques and board of knots. It's so quiet without anyone else there. In one corner there are three cotton shirts hung by a hanger from a peg, and the storeroom door is open.

They sit on wooden chairs with some biscuits on a plastic yellow plate between them. Willy helps himself to two, and pours another drink. His chair is directly opposite a fireplace whose bricks are covered with fine yellow dust. It's just like his fireplace at home, with dust that grows all summer, and makes his mother sneeze.

'You like riding your bike?'

Willy thinks from the way Tan says this that maybe he's seen him riding past the hall before. He says, 'It's okay.' Then he blurts out, 'I'm not very good at sport. Like the sports teacher said I've got two left feet.' He grins, but Tan's face is blank. 'I like riding, except it gets too hot. I'd rather go to Dickson pool.' He stares at Tan, who leans back, stretching his legs out. Willy notices his smooth oval calf muscles with hardly any hairs on them; nothing like his father's legs.

Tan folds his hands behind the back of his head and smiles. 'You are good bike rider. Maybe we ride together some day?'

'Cool, dude!' Willy cries. Then he jumps up. 'Hey! Maybe it's late! Have you got a watch?'

Tan shakes his head, still smiling. He has a smooth kind of smile, which seems to start from his slanted eyes, and move down his face.

'Hey, I've gotta go, man! Be seein' ya!' Willy's not sure why he's suddenly in a hurry, but it feels as though he should be. He pauses at the door. 'Hey! Will you be here tomorrow?' Tan nods. 'Be seein' ya then! Bye!'

Riding home, Willy feels the dog days lift off him, just rise and float away.

———————

'Have you got your bike Tan? Tan! How about we go for a ride today?'

'I have bike!' Tan cries, his face lighting up in greeting. 'Wait there!' He appears quickly around the corner of the cub hall, wheeling a beaten looking bike. It has straight handlebars, like Willy's, but the paint's practically gone; what's left is faded to a rusty colour which might have been red.

Tan smiles and says, nodding towards Willy's shining bike, 'For Christmas, is it?'

'Where'd you get yours?'

'Badger.'

'Come on!' Willy cries, jumping on his bike, and they

head off down the gravel path that crosses the park.

Hot resin and dust rise through their wheels.

Tan rides slowly, glancing across at Willy. 'Where do you live?' he asks.

Willy takes his left hand from the handlebars, and signals vaguely towards Black Mountain. 'Over there,' he says flatly. He gives Tan sidelong looks, then drops back a little so that they're no longer riding abreast. 'Tan,' he whispers, slipping the word under his tongue, wondering what it's like to have a name that means "go brown". When they get to the end of the park, they stop and look at one another. Willy's suddenly self-conscious.

'We go back, is it?' Tan asks, and he nods.

Once again, they sit in the cool hall and drink orange cordial, and eat sweet, crumbly biscuits.

'Can I see your room Tan? Where you sleep and that?'

Tan gathers up the plates and mugs, saying, 'I have bed in the storeroom. Badger have fix it for me. Badger is very good man.'

Willy opens his mouth to ask where Tan will go on cub nights when cubs starts again, but another question comes out. 'Where're your mother and father?'

'In China.'

Willy's never properly looked at anybody Chinese before. When Tan smiles his eyes get smaller, yet his smile does definitely seem to start from them.

'Tan! Knock knock!' Willy cries.

Tan smiles and shakes his head.

'It's a knock knock joke. I say knock knock and you say who's there? Knock knock.'

'Who is there?'

'Stan.'

Tan looks at Willy and waits.

'Stan who? That's what you say.'

'Stan who?'

'Stan back I'm going to sneeze!'

Willy does an enormous achoo, holding his sides and rolling back from his hips, laughing in hot dry bursts.

———•———

Tan takes photographs of cockatoos, rosellas and galahs in the pine trees. Flocks of cockatoos fly screeching, to land and bicker in the trees closest to the cub hall. Willy's mother says it's the drought — that's why there are so many of them. Willy capers and shouts, 'Over here Tan! This'd make a good one!' As often as not, he frightens the birds before Tan has a chance to point his camera at them. But Tan doesn't mind. One day a yellow-breasted bird that he's never seen before, and that Willy can't identify either, flies into a tree above their heads. Tan has his camera ready and it's a lucky shot; clear, with the dark green pine needles and the blue sky behind it. Tan gets several prints done, and gives one to Willy. He sends another to an address in Beijing, without a signature or any writing at all.

———•———

'Look Tan!' Willy holds out his model pterosaur with both hands. 'You buy the wood bits and stick 'em together. Then I cover mine with papier-mâché and paint 'em. That's extra. Like nobody knows what colour they were, so I paint 'em whatever colour I like. D'*you* like it? Pterosaurs didn't have feathers. They could fly, but. D'you like it Tan? D'you wanna hold him?'

Willy hands the plywood and paper creature to Tan, who takes it carefully. 'Is well made,' he says, smiling at

Willy. He passes a finger gently along the thin reptilian wings, and Willy grins with pride.

'Hey Tan!' he says, after taking his model back and setting it on the kitchen bench, 'wanna come and see all my dinosaurs? I've made a display.'

'Some time,' Tan says. 'Not today. Today I have to go out.'

Willy looks up quickly, wanting to know where, but Tan turns to the fridge and gets out the familiar cordial bottle and takes down a glass. He never leaves food or drink around on the benches, and every surface in the kitchen is wiped clean.

Willy sips his cordial and says, 'I'll give you a lend of my pterosaur, if you like — for one week. If you like.'

Tan thanks him and says he will take good care of it. He hasn't poured himself a drink. He looks expectantly towards the door.

Willy rinses his glass in the sink. He's learnt to do this without being asked, in Tan's kitchen. 'Better be going I s'pose. If you're busy. See ya.'

Tan unexpectedly takes his hand and shakes it up and down, and thanks him again for the loan of the pterosaur.

When Willy's getting ready for bed that night, saying goodnight to each of his dinosaurs in turn, the gap where his pterosaur was seems so big, like it's grown while he was in the bath or something. He feels uneasy and sad — not that he doesn't know Tan'll look after it. It's because his collection's incomplete. He might just drop in tomorrow to check that the pterosaur's okay. He lies in bed, waiting for his mother to finish with Emily and come and kiss him goodnight. He thinks of his pterosaur in the dark cub hall. Will Tan take it into the storeroom with him? He should have shown Tan how to hang it so that it looks like it's flying. He imagines a real pterosaur flying round the cub hall on its great wings. And the cub hall's a cage. It'll have to fold its wings right away to get out of the door! He used to believe that it was possible for humans to go back to the time of the dinosaurs. He and Alex, who's still away down the coast, used to have long discussions about it.

When he gets up the next morning and sees that it's raining, Willy asks his mother if he can borrow one of her mixing bowls and boil some water to make steam. She boils the jug herself, half fills a bowl and tells him to carry it carefully. He places it on his desk, under some long fern fronds he's arranged in a milk bottle. His dinosaurs are grazing in a swamp now, plant-eaters closest to the ferns, cropping, chewing. And there's T. Rex and Allosaurus! Run! Run!

All the long dull time while Emily's asleep and he's not allowed to make a noise, Willy sits with his dinosaurs. The water cools in the bowl, and no more steam rises from it. He mustn't disturb his mother by asking for more, or go into the kitchen and do it himself. Though of course he *can* — he's not a baby like Emily; he's not going to drop things or burn himself! He sits and stares at his models, and imagines the rain on the window falling into his swamp, replenishing it, soaking animals and plants, turning the ground mushy under heavy feet. He hears a faint scratching. It's the feet of small mammals huddled under rocks, damp and waiting. Ferns and cycads arch above his head. He's an insect. Or yes! An early mammal, rat-like, defenceless yet safe, fast enough and smart enough, living his life in the shadows of ancient giants, aware of danger every time he looks up, or runs out of his hole in the rocks to look for food — aware of danger with his whole body, as a human boy is not. This is why, thinks Willy, if he ever *is* transported back to dinosaur time, he will run and run, and he will escape.

———•———

For Willy, riding all the way to Fyshwick is like being in the middle of a hot, horrible maze, like his town plan for bicycles gone totally arse-about. Tan looks to his right and left, then slides across the main streets, riding with his knees stuck out the sides — he says this makes it cooler. Willy looks quickly to the right and left, then sort of slugs across after him.

Car after car, trucks, buses, semi-trailers, pass far too close. Once a taxi forces Willy into the gutter, and he skids and nearly comes off. A lot of the traffic is in a hurry to get out of Canberra, to towns and cities further on. Fyshwick, where they're headed, Willy's always thought of as being out of Canberra, out of the main city and different, because no-one lives there. He's been to Fyshwick once with his father to buy second-hand furniture, and once to the half-case warehouse. He has a clear memory of these visits in the car, when he could lean back in his seat and watch as they passed shop after shop, small factories, places that sold wood, and used cars, all crammed up against each other, dwarfed by their own advertisements, with no space for trees or anything in between.

Now Willy feels as though he's being held under a hot tap, only it's dust coming out, not water, and it's too late to tell Tan about his promise to his mother to stay on the bike path. He's almost too tired to see when Tan stops at a corner, and points ahead to where a new building is going up. A half-finished brick wall is closest to them, and wooden scaffolding past that, then heaps of orange dirt and broken rock.

Willy gets off his bike and lets it fall to the ground. He stumbles and shades his eyes. 'There Tan? Is that the place?'

'I think so, yes.' Tan is already striding forward. There doesn't seem to be anybody about, no trucks, no men with tools. They've come all through Fyshwick and out the other side; and there's nothing in front of this new building but sloping grass and stones, down to the Molonglo.

Willy picks up his bike again, hauls it a few steps, and leans it against the partly built wall. He undoes the chain, and chains the two wheels together.

Tan is squatting on his haunches by a pile of rocks. He takes a small hammer out of his pocket, picks up one of the rocks and cradles it in his hand for a moment before lifting the hammer and, without seeming to apply any force at all, deftly breaks the rock down the middle. He stares at the two halves.

'What is it? What's there?' Willy cries, leaping over to him.

'I do not know English name,' Tan says in an odd, strained voice.

'But it's important? It's something? Can I have a go?'

Tan hands him the hammer, and walks off by himself further down the hill. Willy picks up a small rock, balances it narrow side up against a larger, flattish one, and hits it with the hammer. The first time he misses, but the second time the rock splits, and he bends excitedly over the pieces. On the inside of one, there's the indentation of a shell, fan-shaped, yellower than the rock around it.

'Tan!' Willy yells. 'I've got one!' He goat-leaps down

the hill, over stones and clumps of paper-dry grass.

'Well done, Willy!' Tan thumps him on the back, holding the fossil right up close to his face to examine it, and smiling his old smile.

After this, everywhere Willy looks there are fossils. He only has to pick up a rock, tap it, and a new one comes to light. He blushes when he remembers his mistake, thinking they were going to look for dinosaur bones.

Tan explains that the remains of these little animals are much older than the dinosaurs, four times as old, and that, at the time they lived, all the land around them was under the sea.

'Cowabunga!' Willy says in an awed voice. 'You mean Canberra? Canberra was under the sea?'

Tan nods.

'You should've worn a hat. You wanna borrow mine for a while?'

'A hat, yes,' Tan says flatly. 'I forget him.'

'I still wish we could find just *one* dinosaur bone,' Willy says softly, glancing at Tan from under his eyebrows, expecting him to laugh. But Tan nods seriously and agrees that it would be wonderful.

'How come you know so much about fossils and stuff?' Willy asks when they've filled their plastic bags, and are sitting in the narrow shade cast by the half brick wall to drink their fruit juice and eat their apples.

'It was my study at home,' Tan says patiently, but also as if he somehow expected Willy to know this.

'At home? You mean in China?'

'At Beijing University. But we went to different parts, digging and so on.' Tan pretends to dig, with his hands by his sides. 'There is much work —'

'When you go home? You'll do it then?' Willy prompts.

Tan stares straight ahead, and a warning note comes into his voice. 'Perhaps. Perhaps I will.'

But Willy won't be put off this time. 'Have you been in trouble with the police? Tan! Have you been stealing gold watches?'

Tan looks out over Willy's head, and his voice is hard. 'Trouble,' he said.

Willy leans forward and says, 'Tan! How come you live in the cub hall? I mean really?'

Tan says quietly, 'I tell you some time Willy, not now.'

Willy nods. Once he told Alex a secret, at any rate a private piece of information which Alex helpfully blabbed to the whole of grade three.

Tan takes a packet of toothpicks out of his pocket and begins to pick his teeth with one. 'Tell me — what is it like, your dinosaurs' time?'

'Well —' Willy begins.

'You like to go back there, to that time? You believe too, is it?'

Willy feels uneasy, in case Tan's pulling his leg. Then he grins. 'Trouble! A tasty little human morsel. Chomp! Chomp!' He grinds his teeth and pretends to take a bite out of his arm.

Tan smiles and Willy begins chattering then, at the top of his voice, delighted to have someone who'll listen. 'T. Rex'll go for me and I'll dodge, like this! And run!' Willy does karate chops with his hands. Tan laughs and covers his head in mock fear. Willy begins to run around Tan in a skittering circle, faster and faster, until his legs crumple and he collapses in a heap.

———•———

Emily's rash, which has begun to get better, flares up

again and their mother bangs cupboard doors and shouts. She goes to the clothesline to bring in tinder dry clothes she's hung out less than an hour before, and shakes her fist at the untroubled sky. Willy's father is away on a work trip. His mother says he can go to Dickson pool with Tan.

Willy hoots and shouts 'Cowabunga dude!' and hugs her. She rolls backwards and forwards on the balls of her feet, and laughs for the first time in days.

Willy can swim a length of the big pool, just. He watches Tan lower himself into the shallow end and jumps in, water shooting up his nose. Tan stands with his shoulders hunched, squinting against the noise and press of children's bodies.

'Watch me!' Willy shouts. 'Watch me Tan!' He strikes out for the deep end. His beginning is too vigorous and show-off and he's tired by half way. He dog paddles and looks round to see if he can spot Tan. And there he is! On the side, out of the water! Waving and making swimming movements. 'Come on Willy!' Willy can just hear his voice.

He makes it to the end, grabs hold of the bar and looks up grinning into Tan's delighted face. 'You good swimmer Willy! Good swimmer!'

'Jump in!'

Tan straightens and shakes his head. 'Not here.' He lifts his chin towards the shallow end. 'It's better.'

Willy tosses up whether or not to swim back, decides he won't, and glides to the steps with a couple of easy underwater strokes. They muck about for a while at the shallow end, and Willy shows off again, swimming under Tan's legs. He grabs Tan by the foot and Tan yells and waves his leg about madly, while Willy hangs on underwater till his breath gives out, then he breaks the surface, laughing fit to burst.

'My shout, dude,' Willy says importantly, rummaging under his towel for the two dollars tied in a hanky that his mother gave him.

They walk across the damp grass to the kiosk, Tan with his arm around Willy's shoulders. And that's when Willy sees it. How could he have missed such a scar? White and curved, red at the edges, all down Tan's side and around to his back. Willy puts out a finger and touches it, the scar ridge. Tan freezes. Willy feels a shudder go right through the man and then through him, catching them like a wave underwater.

'Don't!' Tan claps his arm to his side.

Willy takes a step backwards, his finger stinging where he's touched the scar. 'What *happened*?' Some kids carrying ice-creams crash into him and keep going. Tan's just standing there with his shoulders hunched and his arms stiff.

'Come on,' Willy says at last. 'Y' don't hafta tell me if you don't want to. What'll you have?' He points to the board above the kiosk's counter. 'We've got two dollars. I'm gunna have a rainbow Billabong. Tan?'

Tan studies the ice-cream advertisements. Each has its price underneath in print large enough for a child to read at a distance. There's a queue four deep waiting to be served. After what seems an age to Willy, Tan says, 'I think a Billabong for me also.'

———— ·—·—— ————

Willy's glad when school goes back, but the bad bit is that Alex and Robert are both in the other grade four, Mrs Reimer's, and he's in crabby Mrs Bennett's. Not only that, but both their families have been down the coast together and now they're best friends. They tell Willy to get lost and won't even speak to him.

On the night of the first cub meeting for the year, it's raining cats and dogs. 'It's raining cats and dogs,' Willy's father says. 'I'll have to drive you.'

'Dad!' Willy cries. 'What's worse than raining cats and dogs?' His father opens his mouth to say he doesn't know. Willy shouts and jumps in the air. 'Hailing taxis! Dad! D'ya get it? Dad!'

Willy holds his sides and roars laughing, until his father says, 'Stop it. You'll make yourself sick.'

Outside the cub hall, he tumbles out of the car, grabbing his fifty cent sub from his father's hand, almost dropping it in a puddle in his rush. He stares down at the puddle for a moment, watches as it grows amazingly, swallowing dust.

Half-a-dozen boys are jumping up and down under the pine trees, faces lifted to the rain. Willy glances back towards his father's car, then rushes up to them. One's got a yo-yo. He's not using it like you should, but flinging it out around his head, tied to his finger by a loop in the string, making the other boys duck. Willy throws his head back and squeezes his eyes shut, pretending not to see the yo-yo coming, then ducks at the very last minute. The cool steady rain tickles his face.

And there's Tan at the window! 'Tan!' Willy yells, waving. He rushes inside. The storeroom door's closed. He calls softly, 'Tan?' There's a scraping sound, and Tan opens the door.

Willy stares into the room. There's a camp bed under the window, with a pillow at one end and a folded rug at the other. You can see the marks where Tan's been standing on the bed to look out the window, not dirty or anything; a crumple. There's a piece of material with Chinese writing on it pinned to one wall. The ropes and brooms and buckets are all there, shoved up one end.

Tan says, 'Hello Willy.'

Willy feels that things have got out of order somehow. He blurts out, 'Why aren't you at your work?'

'Oh well.' Tan shrugs, taking a step backwards, away from the door, and glancing behind him as an enormous shout goes up outside. 'They don't want me anymore. Some new cleaners are there.'

'Willy!' a voice calls. It's Akela. Willy pokes his head round the door, but can't see the cub leader anywhere.

'Hey Tan, why do dinosaurs have serrated tails? From standing too close to the pencil sharpener!' Willy lets out a hoot of laughter. 'Tan, you know what?' he says quickly. 'Our new teacher looks like a German shepherd. She looks like a sheep dog.'

Tan smiles and shakes his head. 'You be smart boy, do good at school.'

There's Akela's voice, louder this time. 'Willy!'

Willy glances apologetically at Tan, who smiles and makes a little pushing movement with his hands, as if to say, hurry.

Willy mumbles 'See you', and rushes to see what Akela wants.

It's just to look after a new chum, show him where things are and that.

Willy says importantly, 'Like you can't wear your uniform till you get invested, but you can get your mum to buy it for you. But like, you won't have any badges or anything. I've got a cooking badge, and a badge for planting trees and —'

'Have ya got any for tying knots?'

'Nah. I can tie heaps of knots but. A reef knot's really cool, there's nothing to it, just right over left and left over right. Want me to show you?'

'Nah. Well, maybe.'

'Hey! I could tie a reef knot round myself and try to get out! Like Houdini!'

The new chum grins.

———•———

They form a circle for the closing ceremony. Willy swallows with pride when he sees Tan watching from the storeroom doorway. Red six, Willy's six, leads off. Willy folds the flag well, without getting the edges crooked the way he sometimes does. He watches Akela out of the corner of his eye, knowing Akela's in the mood to pounce on every little mistake; but it all goes off without a hitch. Back in his place in the circle for the prayer, Willy looks at Tan once again. Tan's face is lifted towards the ceiling, sort of flat towards the light, with his eyes half closed.

'Willy!' Akela reminds him, and Willy obediently pulls off his cap and lowers his eyes for prayer. Then there's the quick last order, 'Pack dismissed!' and the boys rush for the door.

Willy badly wants to talk to Tan, but Akela's there before him, nodding and moving his arms up and down with a quick, no-nonsense, slicing action. Willy can't see Tan's face — and there are three or four boys around Akela, waiting their turn to speak to him. Willy takes a few steps towards the door and waves to Tan, trying to catch his attention. Tan looks like he's listening to every word Akela says, like it must be important.

Willy doesn't know why he should feel let down. His

father's waiting in the car. The rain has stopped and the sky over the Black Mountain is the colour of bruised roses. He says yes, no and okay Dad, in answer to his father's questions. He decides Tan must really have had something important to say to Akela, something he had to keep present in his mind while he was waiting for cubs to finish. He remembers the few occasions when he's had to give a message to Akela, how he went over the message in his head so he wouldn't forget it, and on one occasion it came out wrong and Akela barked at him that he wasn't making sense. He remembers this incident because the sense of the message left him at once and completely at that moment, and he was unable to go over it and get it right.

———•———

The big boys are in a huddle under the pine trees when Willy arrives on the night of the second cub meeting — in a circle with their heads together. Willy only catches a few words before they fling themselves apart, laughing. 'Vandals!' Willy hears. An older boy shouts, 'One two three woof!' And another, 'On the roof, Akela said!' Two of them begin chasing a third, who zigzags through the trees, too fast for them. Akela comes to the door of the cub hall and calls out that they're about to start.

Willy grabs an arm on the way in and asks, 'What vandals, man?'

'Here the other night,' the boy hisses over his shoulder.

Willy keeps looking towards the storeroom door, hoping Tan will come out for the closing ceremony like he did last time. But the door remains shut. Willy thinks he hears a radio coming from inside, but he can't be sure.

'Who is it, telling these things?' Tan wants to know. 'You boys have got some crazy story, is it?'

'No Tan! The vandals are real! You must've seen them Tan! They've been up on the roof!'

Willy props in front of the fireplace with his hands on his hips. 'You scared them away Tan. Akela said!'

Tan walks away from Willy, to take something off the stove. Willy rubs sweaty hands on his T-shirt, and wonders if he could get himself a glass of cordial. He's called by after school on impulse. He had to find out about the vandals.

'I know what we'll do!' he cries. 'We'll set a trap for them! When they come we'll run out and capture them! It'll have to be at night, at midnight!' Willy's eyes itch with a pleasant scary feeling.

It won't be so hard to catch the vandals once they're inside the hall, because it's only got one outside door. Inside there are — how many separate rooms? Willy ticks them off on his fingers. The kitchen and the storeroom, the bathroom and toilet and the main room. There's the fireplace and chimney. The vandals might try and escape up the chimney. Will they have guns?

'Badger says —' Tan begins, turning round and looking out over the top of Willy's head with a queer flat look, like he's miles away.

'We'll wait at night! They'll be coming back at night Tan!'

Tan lowers his head then, and his eyes focus on Willy, who remembers the scar underneath his T-shirt, the red and white scar curving halfway across his back.

Tan says, 'Be a smart boy okay? Not getting into trouble.'

'My dad's away again.' Willy begins to explain about his mother and father — but it's pointless. He says, 'You can't stop me. You can't cut me out of this Tan? Please?'

He spends the whole evening, at home, puzzling over the vandals and how to trap them. His mother gives him surprised looks and says, 'Well, it's nice and peaceful for a change.'

He listens outside his mother's door, to make sure she's asleep. It's possible that, if Emily wakes up, she'll check on him too. So he bundles some clothes under the sheet to look like it's him sleeping. A sheet by itself is not terribly good cover, but the night's too hot for blankets. He has to rely on his mother not coming right into the room, just looking through the door. Before dark, he took his bike out of the shed and wheeled it to the back gate. He didn't want to be fiddling round in the shed, and maybe knock something over.

His mother seems sound asleep, he can hear her breathing anyhow. He checks the time on the digital clock with the big luminous numbers. He's worried in case the vandals make their move before midnight. He opens the back door and lets himself out, his running shoes silent on the concrete.

The hot wind comes at him, first from the side then from behind, nearly toppling the bike. He wobbles across the footpath, wind blowing hair and grit into his mouth. He spits and keeps his head well down. He can't lock the back gate from the outside, but makes sure it's shut. He switches his light on. He likes the whirring sound the dynamo makes on his front wheel. He shivers and wishes Alex and Robert could see him now. He feels as light as anything, inside — weightless.

He taps with his knuckles on the door of the cub hall

and calls softly, 'Tan. It's me Willy.' The hall's in total darkness. He calls again. 'Tan!'

He hears a sound at the storeroom window, then footsteps behind the door. The door opens a crack.

'Hi! I made it.'

Tan grips him by the arm. 'Willy! Go!'

'Ow! You're hurting me!' Willy pushes past Tan, into the hall. 'Quick, shut the door! Have they come yet?'

'Go home,' Tan says sharply. 'You go home!'

Willy ignores him and heads for the kitchen. 'We'll wait in here. Good thing you remembered to turn off all the lights.'

Tan sighs then, and sits down heavily on one of the wooden chairs.

A strong rush of wind circles the cub house. 'Maybe we'll get a hurricane?' Willy says quickly. 'Or a tornado?' He listens to the wind, with his head first on one side, then the other. Suddenly there's a different noise. He waits, and it comes again, like someone scratching on the guttering.

There's a fall of stones against the kitchen window. Willy jumps to his feet and tries to hoist himself onto the bench by the sink. Tan pulls him roughly down by the legs. 'Ow,' Willy hisses. 'You're hurting me!'

'Sit down!' Tan pulls Willy towards a chair. 'Don't move!'

Tan leaves the kitchen, and Willy hears him moving softly around the big room.

There it is again! Willy jumps in his chair, cranes his neck. It's scary in the kitchen by himself. He tiptoes to the door and peers around the big room. It's very dark. Tan's not there, so he must be in the storeroom. Willy's too scared to go in there after him, so he waits by the door. His eyes focus on the law and promise, fixed to the back wall on their wooden plaque. They shine dully in the darkness, too dim to read, but he knows them off by heart — they're the first things a new chum has to learn. 'On my honour I promise to do my best to serve . . .'

Tan startles Willy when he appears in the doorway, moving on soundless feet. Then there's a noise right over their heads — footsteps. A voice shouts, 'Go home, slit-eyes! We don't want no chink bastards here!'

Tan stands very still. Willy thinks — what if the vandals are coming down the chimney? He pulls on Tan's arm. 'The chimney Tan!' Tan just stands there, like he's deaf or something. Willy runs past him to the fireplace. The noises sound like they're all over the roof now. He crawls into the fireplace and tries to look up the chimney. He puts his hands up for balance and dislodges some soot, which falls in his eyes, making them sting. He hunches his shoulders up to his ears. The noises on the roof have stopped.

Tan's standing where Willy left him, arms stiff by his sides.

'Tan!' Willy whispers, grabbing his sleeve. 'The van-dals'll get away!'

When Tan won't move, Willy runs across the big room and into the storeroom. He climbs onto Tan's bed and peers out the window. He can see the concrete step in front of the door, and the gravel space around it, up to the first of the pine trees. There's no-one there. Then he hears a different noise, not loud footsteps on the roof, but a clunking sound. He jumps off the bed and backs away from the window. There's a noise of something landing on the gravel.

For a few seconds everything stops and there's the weirdest silence — the wind stops circling the house — the noises near the chimney stop, and even the voice inside Willy's head. He waits till he feels he can't wait anymore, then moves towards the bed again, not standing on it this time, but crouching, then very carefully lifts his head so that it's level with the window ledge.

There's something bright on the ground. At first Willy has no idea what it is. Then he recognises it — it's a burning branch. The flames burn right along it, then quiver and begin to die down. Willy's neck and shoulders ache. He doesn't ask himself whether it's safe to go out — he only knows that's what he has to do now. Quietly, he walks to the main door, pulls back the bolt and opens it. It shuts with a click behind him.

He glances down at the burning branch on the step. There's no danger there; it will soon burn itself out. Then he hurries round the corner to where he's parked his bike. Between one breath and the next he's on it, and away.

———◆———

All next day the wind blows hot and strong, exhausting people and animals without exhausting itself. Willy's back door has a large gap underneath it. Dust and bits of twigs and leaves sweep in, messing up the laundry floor, until Willy's mother gets an old bit of blanket, rolls it up, and shoves it against the door. She hasn't taken Emily outside for days, only making short dashes to the clothes-line and back, to bring in nappies that are stiff dry, with a mustard coating of dust. She says that if the wind doesn't stop soon she'll go mad, and Willy believes her.

He doesn't want to go to school. He feels scared and

tired; he'd like to be a baby again, and just go back to bed. His mother pushes him out the door and he walks along the footpath with his head bent and his school bag clamped to his chest. He is scared of school, and scared of home. For those few minutes, dragging his feet against the weight of wind, he's even scared of himself.

At three in the afternoon he's so tired he can scarcely keep his eyes open. He drops his bag in the hallway, calls out 'Mum — I'm home,' goes straight to his room and lies down. The next thing he knows is his mother's calling him for dinner.

Emily sways from side to side in her high chair and posts bits of food in the pocket of her plastic bib. Willy feeds her with a spoon and she giggles and copies his exaggerated chewing, swinging her jaws from side to side. 'Little monkey,' Willy says and tickles her behind the ear.

It's only after they've cleaned up, and Willy's taking the garbage out the back that he sees red in the sky and smells smoke.

The whole park is on fire. As soon as Willy crosses the road, he's surrounded by it. Trees bright as suns, between them twisting smoke shadows, everywhere he looks. 'Tan!' he shouts at the top of his voice. 'I'm coming Tan!' He drops his bike on the path and continues on foot, arms across his face now, elbows out. The heat pushes him back, like a door being slammed in his face, but *he* pushes *it*, leans against it with all his strength and pushes forward. Sparks swat his face, a branch hits his shoulder and he twists, shrugs it off, all the time calling Tan's name.

Now the noise of the fire and falling branches is so loud he can hardly hear himself. The shadows behind and around him are too big for men; they're the shadows of lost giants, wailing as the flames eat them. Willy stumbles forward a few more steps, then sees Tan, standing as still as if frozen in time, staring at what used to be the cub hall, but is now an orange wall from ground to skyline.

'Tan!' Willy runs forward and grabs the man's arms, pulls him back along the gravel path. Tan stares at Willy, his flat face registering nothing; but he doesn't resist, he allows himself to be dragged away from the gutted building.

A few yards down the path, a fallen tree bars their way, and Willy hesitates, then, still pulling Tan along, leaves the path and zigzags between the trees, making for the shortest way out of the park. He thinks once, briefly, of his bike abandoned on the gravel. He doesn't stop or speak until he's through the last of the trees, and across the melting bitumen, then his legs fold under him and he starts to cry.

Ha Ha Ha!

NICHOLAS JOSE

His grandmother saw the empire collapse, the presidency fail, the republic overthrown and successive communist regimes slide into madness or corruption. In her ninety-five years she had learned one thing — in a crisis governments always make the wrong decision. She had no faith in the capacity of human beings to run the world. It was enough to survive, accepting advantage when offered, resisting the step that leads into danger. Her grandson, the artist, inherited these attitudes. Large, slow and jolly, he was seldom quick to seize an opportunity, but never blind to benefits deserved. He grew up in part of an old courtyard house, a populated world within a maze of rooms and passages within the security of four walls in the old city. No need to fly the cosy nest in search of sustenance or stimulation. The other birds were fat and heavy, bundled up in padded clothes for most of the year, stuffed full of stories, sayings, and eccentric ingrained habits. They were the people who inhabited his paintings.

Picking their noses and farting foully, with weak hearts and yellowed teeth, they were far from heroes. They fiddled the weights and measures, when flour or oil was distributed, delighted in children and criticised negligent parents behind their backs. They laughed, gossiped, plotted and, in later years, grew bent with weariness. Each new season, each arrival or departure, each new slogan, they greeted with hope — the most eccentric habit of all.

The artist married and moved into a new apartment in a high-rise block, with much improved amenities and a cooler geometry, grey and cellular. New artistic influences came in, which he digested with an iron stomach, like the strongman who chomps his way through engine parts. Cubism, surrealism, constructivism, abstract expressionism, conceptual art. His people, unchanged in themselves, came to inhabit a different environment in his pictures. They took off their clothes, revealing roly-poly bodies that danced. They stood on their hands, wiggled their genitals, and held their fingers in the gestures of Peking opera. In bright confusion their eyes peered from featureless faces.

Because he could not make his people into heroes, giants to glorify the national soul, he was refused entry to art school and the noble designation of state artist. Sent to teach kids in a middle school, he amused them with his idea that art was play.

He painted a world full of nonsense. Curious foreigners, who laughed bitterly at the pudgy, pottering figures of the courtyards, came to visit him, intrigued by work which had the power to tenderise. Deflecting envy and slander, he became a guide to other artists. He loved to pontificate on the great themes of culture, history and humanity. Understanding by no means all he said, artists, critics and foreign patrons, diplomats and journalists, stopped to listen to the plump bird in his feathered nest.

'Ha ha ha!' he would laugh, innocently appreciating the ridiculous, 'hee hee hee!' In his bubbling, effortless laughter, part wit, part outflow of sheer pleasure, he was free.

His world began with the centre of gravity in his lower belly that tied him to the earth, focussing and balancing his large body. Taller and bigger boned than almost everyone else, he was a great bear. Next after himself came his wife, parents, sisters, brothers and mates, tied to his belly as if by umbilical cords. The people beyond were unknown and shadowy, perhaps inimical. If they could not be ignored, they were best treated decorously. Officials, watchmen, neighbourhood busybodies, buyers and sellers, bureaucrats. Among his friends he was the laughing chairman, bestowing marks for bold behaviour.

It was a time for trying on new ideas, new ways of acting, for creative fantasy, and fantastic creation, with no-one knowing where it would lead. From the coal-dust stained walls and tiles of the courtyard nests flight to the moon was possible, and he painted the comedy of his ungainly people lifting off, like hydrogen-filled blimps, into ever wider orbits among the stars. He was visited by ambassadors, reproduced in fashionable magazines. His style became a contagion, laughing enthusiasm, sardonic ridicule, deep fantasy that fired the blood. His exhibition opened on the day the citizens swarmed into the streets, seeing invisible signals of a new beginning, protesting in excited hundreds of thousands against the state of their world. They paraded into the square in front of the palace in yellow party dresses with black polka dots, in tight shorts and turquoise sports shirts and plastic sandals, in jeans and defiant home-made headbands. They pranced and waved their arms, turning and advancing as on a stage, with their fingers making the gestures of Peking opera, the same gestures as international rock stars performing for the poor of the Earth. V for Victory, V for Peace, V for Freedom. On the walls of the gallery his people paraded in a similar dance, on tiptoes, defying gravity, through the repeated grey columns and nonsensical red markers that defined their space.

The parade was washed away in blood, as a storm breaks over a holiday, sending picnickers scattering like bedraggled birds. Gaiety and colour mired in the gutter, balloons exploded, jam sandwiches were smeared in the dirt for ants to crawl over before they too were squashed or drowned. Those who stepped out of their courtyards to see what was happening took one step too many and became participants. Those who came down from high-rise balconies to get a better look found themselves shot by stray bullets. Some who proclaimed 'Dare to Die!' died. Others crawled on their bellies to survive. People whom the aura of idealism protected like invisible armour were caught in the path of tanks, the rain of crossfire, tripped by their own frailty, and became the uncountable dead of the night of the massacre.

He painted their portraits and hid them under the bed, the flesh of their red-crayon faces flaking like courtyard walls, their grins turning to gallows grimaces, turning to howls.

When he and his friends met, several stories up, behind

locked doors, to eat dumplings in a hot, smoke-filled room, while outside in the grey city heads were cowed and faces passed blankly, with fear, shame, anger and the shifts of survival in the autumn air, they formed a manifesto to allow their creative fantasy to continue in the corner that was left. The sapling was transplanted to a tiny pot of compost mixed with shards.

They produced work from whatever materials were available, catching ideas that gusted past like leaves. Wind. String. Frame. Photograph. The game had rules. Each artist would present the work with a little speech, then a secret ballot would take place, in a serendipitous parody of impossible democracy, and prizes would be awarded for first, second and third. The closed circle admitted no strangers, but each time one would bring a friend, and the numbers grew. After the serious business, they cleared away the artworks and set to feasting. Trooping home, down flights of unlit concrete stairs to the muddy yard, dispersing into the darkness, they were watched by an old woman who sat, knitting in a cardboard box, unobserved. Without any light, she knew when she dropped a stitch.

———•———

The school was quiet after the kids had gone, woodframe windows latched and bolted, doors padlocked. No-one liked to hang around in the low, badly lit buildings. The courtyard was sunless save for a gloomy, lurid late afternoon reflection of sunset, flickering red in the panes of glass. The art room, where he stretched and prepared his canvases, was lit by one bright bulb and warmed by a little electric stove. The door creaked as they swung it open, without knocking, and marched in.

The older man was laughing drily. 'Haven't knocked off yet?'

The artist grunted. He waited for their purpose to be revealed. He knew the face of the older man from around the yard, but had never known his job. The young woman, a good-looking serious type in her early twenties, was a new face.

'You're busy,' the man added, with a touch of accusation. To be busy was to be occupied in activities beyond what was required. *They* were never busy. To have a task to perform meant trouble.

'Ha ha ha!' the artist laughed. 'What do you want?' The woman pouted disapprovingly, then switched to a nervous smile.

'We've got something to discuss with you. We're from the security section.'

Trouble.

'Right you are. Sit down.' Cheerily the artist moved his canvases and gave his visitors a pair of wooden chairs. 'You're new to the school,' he quipped to the girl.

'Miss Yang is our youngest comrade. Now . . .' The man rubbed his hands.

'Would you like some tea?' the artist interrupted. Rinsing out the glasses gave him time.

'Are these your works?'

'Hee hee hee!'

'We hear you're becoming quite popular. You've had more than one exhibition. Foreigners like your paintings. You've been invited to go abroad.'

'Don't overdo it! The school has given me great support.'

'You've been a teacher here for seven years,' said the girl, who had done her best to memorise his file.

'I enjoy the kids.'

'Your leaders don't have any complaints.' The man filtered the tea leaves with his teeth as he sucked the tea. His glossy black hair was dyed, a handsome, expressionless face with a few standard smile lines, such as a poster artist might draw, thin purple lips. The woman had beautiful creamy skin. No wonder the old man was pleased with the new appointment. It would be his avuncular job to train her.

'What are your paintings about?'

'Ha ha ha! You can look at them and see what you like. I've been studying the *Book of Changes*. Ancient Chinese philosophy is full of the most amazing things. You know that thing which takes a sign and makes it heat up the body until it can do cartwheels and finally fly through time, empowered by entry into a land of mirrors.'

The woman frowned. 'It's superstition,' she said. The man didn't react. He was not interested in examining the artworks. Individual expression was the most irrelevant of phenomena. His task was different.

'We would like to congratulate you on your success. You are glorifying our Chinese culture. We would like to help you. Are you a party member?'

'I never got around to it.'

'Are you a member of the Artists Association?'

He giggled. 'That hasn't been possible.'

'We can fix all that up. An artist cannot make it by himself. He needs support. We want to encourage artists. We want to know more about artists and their lives.'

Pulling out a new packet of foreign cigarettes, the man deftly offered one, and the artist accepted with a curt nod. He stretched his mouth wider, blowing smoke through his teeth in a steady spurt of quiet anger, as his interlocutor continued.

'We'd like to know more about you, and your friends,

your artist friends, and the foreigners who mix in your circle. What do you talk about? What are your views on things? That's all. We'd like to become friends with you.'

The artists drew on the cigarette. He understood exactly what the deal was. A surge of acid bit at his normally tough stomach.

'So that's what you wanted to talk about.'

He reacted slowly. The woman piped up. 'We want to be your friend. You could be a famous artist.'

'You're on the threshold of a great career,' repeated the older man cynically.

'Have some more tea?' The artist bent to pour boiling water into their glasses. 'My wife is expecting me at home. Would you be able to call again?'

'Certainly, of course. No problem. It all takes time.'

'I appreciate your concern,' the artist nodded.

'We'll be back in a month.' When the man spoke these words, the woman rose to her feet as if commanded.

They were going.

'Take care,' he called after them.

If he cooperated, they would make his career. And if he didn't? The artist hated choice. To refuse outright would place an indelible black mark in his file that would affect not only himself and his wife, in every aspect of their lives, but also their children, if they had any, and their friends and associates. He would be unreliable, anti-party, anti-people. There would be no end to it. Nothing would be gained from refusing outright. It was not even polite.

But to go along with them — apart from self-disgust, and the inconvenience of entertaining the anxiously expected guests whenever they chose to call, there was the impossibility of satisfying their demands. If he betrayed his friends and revealed to the security section exactly what was done and said, it would amount to little more than a lot of half-baked theories about art, arguments, ambitions, enthusiasms, frustrating attempts to sell paintings to foreigners who might be more willing to buy if the artist expressed some strong anti-government opinions, for the sake of business. Even if he told them everything, it would add little to the information they already had. Did that make betrayal harmless? He would simply be too embarrassed to tell the details of their lives and thoughts. Unable to give what they wanted, he would be pressured for more, and more. Should he invent? What harm in engaging in a bit of play-acting? But they would catch him out. He had known people who tried to equivocate. They kept it up for a while, and got into trouble in the end. There was a false logic in forcing someone to become an informer. Once known, the information had little value. The purpose of the visit was to intimidate him. It was the system's best means of control. And he was more frightened than he had ever been in his life. He should never have stuck his neck out. But he couldn't help it. He was bigger, fatter, taller than the others.

One month later to the day they returned. He looked up surprised, but was ready for them, the same peculiar couple, the older man and the girl. Confident in his handling of the case, the older man was more openly lascivious than the first time, while the woman had become less lovely in her discomfiture. Perhaps the man had already imposed himself on her. The artist poured tea, offered a good, Chinese-made cigarette.

'You're as busy as ever.'

'I don't have much time after I finish teaching.'

'Now about that matter.'

'I put you to so much trouble.'

'We're friends, after all.'

'Friends!'

'You have many friends.'

'I have a few.'

'We'd like to be counted among them.'

'The trouble is my friends must meet certain conditions.'

The older man raised his eyebrows. It was not the victim's place to impose conditions.

'You know the game of go? I've been mad about the game since I was a child. My father taught me when I was six years old and I've been playing ever since. I'm pretty good, even if I do say so myself.'

Black and white counters forming lines and enclosures on a grid, black surrounding white, white encasing black. Go was a game of supreme conceptual simplicity, extreme tactical complexity.

The woman grinned like an idiot. The man stared.

The artist went on. 'My friends can all play go. We spend hours at the game. I'm pretty good, so it's hard for me to find a suitable opponent. My friends have all beaten me on occasions, but usually I beat them. I'm the best. That's the problem. I don't bother playing with people who are not my match.' He laughed. 'Don't think I'm big-noting. It's only a game. It's only go.'

The man from the security section stared, the light leaving his face.

'Would you like a game?' the artist asked keenly. 'Come on. I bet you can play.'

The man froze awkwardly. He waved his hand to indicate that he wouldn't play. He couldn't, or didn't want to — he wouldn't say. His eyes evaded the artist's gaze.

Then he turned to the woman, inviting her to play. But she just laughed. She was paralysed.

'All my friends play go,' said the artist. 'I'm happy to be friends with someone I can play go with. If you can find me someone to beat me at go, I'll be their friend. We can spend hours together. I've been playing since I was six, you see. You must have someone suitable among all your people.'

The artist's eyes twinkled as he blew smoke from the side of his mouth. The man stared straight ahead. His lips became mauve when tight. The woman sat robustly upright. To be taken seriously, they would have to find a go player to match the artist's skill. If the first candidate should lose, they would have to find a second, and a third, and so on. If they continued to lose, it would be a greater shame, a revelation of incompetence and ineffectuality. It were better not to begin.

They would make their report, and pass to higher authorities the responsibility for finding the appropriate person to be involved in the case. Surely someone could be found. It would no longer be their concern, however. Any delays would not be their fault.

'Come back as soon as you find your champion,' said the artist loudly.

His interlocutors stood. They were obliged to take his request seriously. If they ignored his condition, their work lost its legitimacy. No longer concealed behind politeness and decorum, their function would be reduced to simple brutality. They couldn't operate with that admission. They couldn't face it.

They assured him that he would certainly hear from them again soon. After they left, the artist sat on the chair breathing fast.

———————

Another month passed. They never came back. They were reassigned. He never saw their faces again.

He laughed afterwards when he thought of the incident. *Ha ha ha!* It was always possible that one day they would return with their go champion. *Hee hee hee!* He went on getting drunk in the secure circle of his friends. *Ho ho ho!* He never spoke his mind again. Deep he delved into mystic and ancient philosophy, wild theories and mad boasts. Never again did he utter the truth. Talking to him, you knew you were near the facts of the matter when he started to laugh. Ask him point-blank and the response was always the same: *Hee hee hee! Ha ha ha!* You got no more.

The Man Who Knew Walesa

Tom Keneally

Poland, 1982

Polish officials and the troops at the airport wore a rich red kind of khaki and carried nifty little Kalashnikov automatic rifles. To meet this latter-day Polish army, the old Polish warrior Edek Kempner wore his Orbis badge, the badge of the Polish Travel Bureau, and on this afternoon of Polish crisis when the national blood was — as it were — rushing to Bydgoszcz where a farmer had been beaten up, the seas of Polish officialdom nonetheless parted before Edek and his party.

'I said to that son-of-bitch in the uniform,' Edek told his group, while doing business with two porters, one to handle Halinka's luggage, the other to tote that of the three men, 'I tell that son-of-bitch that though I am

American I do lots of work with the Orbis New York office. He asks me what's the address of the New York office. I flabbergast the boychick by telling him 500 Fifth Avenue. I even give him the zip code. He'll check. They check on everything. But Droz who runs the New York office will cover for his old friend Kempner, you better believe it.' He winked, implying some long-standing deal between himself and this Droz, whom Clancy had never met. 'One Pole can wash another Pole's hands.'

They were funnelled through a last barrier. A vast crowd seemed to be waiting for such a small trickle of passengers.

'Most of them are probably spies,' murmured Halinka, the flesh around her eyes having gone blue as if her homecoming had deprived her of oxygen.

And everyone was staring — at the good overcoats of Fodor and Edek, at Halinka's fur, even at the negligent but — by Eastern European norms — affluent clothing of Clancy, the jacket adequate by the standards of a Sydney winter but too thin for Poland, the polo-neck Aran Isle sweater proof against most climates. And of course, they stared at Fodor, for on their soil there had been in the grievous early forties an attempt to expunge dwarfs. 'Should I do a goddamn trick for them?' Fodor asked Clancy.

'Change US dollars in the car park, change US dollars in the car park,' murmured a grey-faced man whom Clancy passed.

'Take no notice,' Fodor advised. 'The motherfucker could be an *agent provocateur.*'

Edek, ahead with the porters, was pounced on out of the crowd by a small man with a bald head and broad Slavic features, the sort of features Clancy was familiar with in Polish emigrants to Australia, the sort of face one saw, the features both hefty and hearty, on road workers, railway guards, cab drivers, in that far south land. Clancy knew it was always the peasants who were likely to travel furthest when they left their homelands — his own grandparents had been Irish peasants. The little ambusher was laughing and had begun to embrace Edek. Within an instant his affection was swallowed in the bear-like arms of Edouard of Beverly Hills.

'You little son of gun,' roared Edek.

His expansiveness terrified some of the crowd this perilous evening and they moved away. Edek sprayed the terminal with affectionate Polish and the little man answered in a self-controlled way, in the way his blood, witness to so many generations of oppression, counselled him. Edek turned to the rest of his party and dragged them into a scrum with the small man he had just embraced. The small man was called Bodgan. He was a Warsaw cab driver to whose family Edek sent food parcels from that company in Chicago who made them up. He was a darling son of a gun and would drive them all round Poland for a few hundred dollars, well maybe three hundred and fifty dollars, which he could then exchange on the open market for about three months wages.

'*Dobry wieczor*,' said Fodor and Halinka.

Clancy tried the same subtle combination of vowels in greeting the cab driver, and Bodgan and his three fellow travellers laughed benignly. It occurred to Clancy, not for the first time, that Polish history — including that *outre* corner of it in which these people had acted — might be as subtle and unachievable to him as were the national vowels.

Outside, in the raw and strange air, Clancy was alarmed by a violent tug on his arm. Turning, he saw it was Halinka, baulked on the pavement. He became aware that her breath was rasping. Her lips parted and a small wail emerged. Bodgan was running merrily to fetch his cab, Edek yelling merrily in his wake and ordering the porters to halt and be patient. Halinka's talons on Clancy's arm seemed to penetrate his clothing. He hoped to tow her, but to his amazement she held him static. The wail grew in volume. Fodor, on the other side of her, fetched her a sharp punch in the kidneys with his gloved hand. Clancy could hear that the blow cut off her breath.

'Come on, sweetie,' said Fodor. 'No-one can touch you. You're a free woman, a citizen of the right half of goddamn Germany.'

Bodgan arrived in his cab, a Mercedes. A suitable vehicle, Clancy thought. Minute Bodgan lashed all Halinka's luggage on the roof-rack. Fodor threw her in the back like a vice cop throwing a prostitute.

As Clancy climbed in, she murmured at him, 'Homecomings? I should not have come. They can sniff my Jewblood and they blame me for the crucified Pole that hangs in every Church.'

'For what it's worth,' said Clancy, taking her bird-like wrist, 'you look like a Frankfurt woman or a New Yorker full stop.'

He knew that the Rist women had not been branded with a tattoo in Auschwitz — they had not been considered permanent enough residents for such treatment. His research told him, too, that when the Jews first came to Kazimierz in Kracow in the fourteenth century, they had resembled the Bedouin, and that only generations of *sub rosa* couplings had made her look so international and Edek look so Polish.

Edek had entered the back of the limo now and taken up the burden of consolation. 'Don't you worry about a thing, darling. You are with Uncle Edek now. One mention of the US Consul and they shit themselves. Believe me, I know the set-up.' He clapped his hands and beamed at Clancy, Fodor, Halinka. 'This is fun! Poland in the spring!'

So they rolled through high-rise suburbs. Clancy looking for signs of the Polish anguish. He pointed to a vast hoarding on one apartment building. 'What does it say?' he asked Edek. Edek translated. 'The parish of Muranow welcomes the Virgin Mary. It's a statue, Clancy. It moves around from parish to parish.'

Clancy thought of the time he had walked three miles in western Sydney to see Father Peyton's statue of the Virgin. The universality of Catholic culture! The foot of the Virgin crushing the serpent both in Warsaw Province and in distant New South Wales.

A public park appeared. 'I performed there once,' said Fodor. 'August of '38. That's when circuses were circuses. People had an honest attitude to freaks. Hitler changed all that. People don't feel comfortable about us any more. I did the stilt act here. Come in on stilts dressed as a member of the goddamn Hapsburg family. Throw off the crown, throw off the ermine, jump off the stilts, and people gasp. What they thought was a prince is a midget. They were the days!'

'Higher wages for higher production,' Edek translated a notice on an overhead bridge. But then Mariology reasserted itself. 'Oh Glorious Virgin, we your servants in Wilanow greet you with love,' proclaimed a banner draped from a construction crane.

'This little fellow,' laughed Edek, reaching through to the front seat and tweaking the ear of Bogdan, 'he knows

Walesa. He knows Klasa in Krakow — you know, Urek Klasa, Walesa's lieutenant down there in my old stamping grounds, my home town. And he knows Wajda the movie-maker and he knows Roman Polanski, that son-of-bitch who does things with children and he knows the other movie-maker, the Krakow man, Blumental, who is a Jew — I used to walk out with his aunt and take her to goddamn patisseries, would you believe?'

Bogdan smiled over his shoulder. Clancy wondered whether it *was* possible that he knew Walesa and the elfin Polanski and Blumental whose film on an electrician's family struggling for economic and spiritual space in one of the suburbs of Krakow had been a hit at festivals in the West.

As if at Edek's invitation, Bogdan the cab driver began talking fiercely. Clancy noticed how intently Fodor and even the barely restored Halinka were listening. Occasionally Edek's *basso* would intrude, a brief translation session for the sake of the Australian. It happened that in the mid-1970s when Bogdan was young and newly married, he had found himself living in the same Gdansk apartment block as Walesa and Walesa's wife and children. He had lost his job as a toolmaker more or less at the same time as Walesa the electrician was sacked by the works committee. He had moved to Warsaw, his wife's city, and taken up with the cab business. It was the best move he could have made, he said (as translated by Edek). You met foreigners who left novels behind in the car — American novels, French novels, novels which delighted his daughter who was training to be a teacher. The other thing the Americans and the West Germans had was a strong currency, but you met Japanese too. The Japanese were wonderful, said Bogdan. They did

things in real style and their generosity earned them
top marks with Warsaw cab drivers. Not that there
was anything wrong with Americans. Americans had top
marks too.

Bogdan struck Clancy therefore as a revolutionary
somewhat neutralised by contact with the right currencies.
Clancy surmised too that nearly everyone in Poland,
exclusive of certain security forces and Party diehards, was
claiming a connection with the phenomenon Walesa. As
if to answer this suspicion, Bogdan flipped the sun visor
above his head downwards — cab drivers often carried
their treasures stuck on the underside of sun visors with
an elastic band. Bogdan extracted a photograph, however,
not from the underside but from a cunning slit in the
leather. He pushed the photograph over his shoulder and
towards Clancy in the back seat. Clancy examined it. It
was a colour photograph some years old, an indoor shot,
and the tile stove, living room wall and other background,
including a framed print of the Sacred Heart of Jesus, had
taken on a coppery tint as if oxidised by all the reverent
hands which touched it. There were two youngish and
anciently Slavic women in the photograph, a younger
Bogdan with more hair, and the unmistakable square
features and droopy moustache of a young Lech Walesa.
'Lescek live at apartment five,' Bogdan explained. 'I live at
apartment seven. One . . . *klorym* . . .'

He gestured upwards with an index finger. Edek again
tweaked the driver's cheek. 'This gorgeous little guy
lived one floor up from Walesa.' He began grilling
Bogdan in Polish and conveying the information to
Clancy. 'The photograph is 1972. Bogdan and Walesa
represented the same work section on the workers council at the shipyard. Did you see his little wife in the

photograph? She's adorable!' *Adorable* was an adjective to which Edek gave a luscious emphasis, pronouncing the second syllable *doo-er*.

Bogdan continued to tell his story in Polish. Edek Kempner continued to translate. Bogdan had worked as a welder in the transport section of the shipyards, a fairly remote depot out near the Dead Vistula to which they sent troublemakers. Walesa had been an electrician, Bogdan a welder side-tracked to delivering truck engines to some further workshop in that enormous industrial region. One day in the autumn of '78 the management told the works council that Lech Walesa had to go. The workshop manager did his best to stand up for Lech but knew it was his job too on the line. The section supervisor refused to act on the dismissal and was demoted to become a storeman. A week later Bogdan and another Walesa lieutenant were sacked. (Edek conveyed all this with plentiful reference to son-of-bitch tyrants.) It is hard enough being on a skilled worker's wage in Poland, Edek translated. To be unemployed is madness and hell.

Clancy imagined a bleak Baltic industrial-scape, a milieu bearable only if one were relating to it with a welding torch, a rivetting gun, or the controls of a crane. Bogdan said Walesa was unabashed by his dismissal. He went on sticking up posters, and when an engineer at the Stennecka Street workshops tore down one of them and was later injured by a turbine engine which fell out of its tackle, Lescek visited the man in hospital and said, 'God punished you, because we put the truth up on the wall and you tore it down. Don't tear down the truth again!'

Bogdan confessed through his interpreter Edek that he himself did not have such certainty about the direct hand of God in Polish affairs. His sacking had frightened the stuffing out of him. God and His Blessed Mother were to be thanked for Bogdan's father-in-law, whom until then Bogdan had considered something of a social parasite, a Warsaw dealer who seemed to be able to travel to West Germany frequently and take plenty of Carmel cigarettes with him. The Polish cigarette had for some reason always been in vogue in Western Europe — now more than ever due to Lescek's popularity, no matter how misunderstood he might be on the international scene. I mean, Lescek is a Pole. He is not some Hollywood movie's idea of a Pole, he is not the CIA's idea of a Pole, he is not a Frenchperson's idea of a Pole. He is a Pole. Forever. That aside, Bogdan's father-in-law had made it possible for him to own his own taxi in Warsaw. I am more comfortable as a cab driver, said Bogdan through Edek. Cab drivers are outside history and so they live through it. Lescek knows this and forgives me for it, Bogdan boasted. Lescek would like a quiet life too, but there is a Polish demon in him.

Halinka's talon grabbed Clancy's wrist. 'They're talking just like they did in the thirties,' whispered Halinka, the sound seeming to come from her stark eyes. 'Demons aren't enough for them. They have to be *Polish* demons. They are awful people. Why did I come, Mr Clancy?'

Clancy thought it best to pat the stick-like wrist behind Halinka's claw. Besides, through Bogdan, he was one flight of stairs up from what every Australian desired — History: the centre.

A darkness had fallen. Street lights pocked but did not dispel it. Suddenly Edek screamed, 'The Vistula! The Vistula!'

'River of such tears,' murmured Halinka, lighting another cigarette.

The Shoes of the Fisherman

―――

MORRIS WEST

The Pope was dead. The Camerlengo had announced it. The master of ceremonies, the notaries, the doctors had consigned him under signature into eternity. His ring was defaced and his seals were broken. The bells had been rung throughout the city. The pontifical body had been handed to the embalmers so that it might be a seemly object for the veneration of the faithful. Now it lay, between white candles, in the Sistine Chapel with the noble guard keeping a death watch under Michelangelo's frescoes of the last judgement.

The Pope was dead. Tomorrow the clergy of the Basilica would claim him and expose him to the public in the Chapel of the Most Holy Sacrament. On the third day they would bury him, clothed in full pontificals, with a mitre on his head, a purple veil on his face, and a red ermine blanket to warm him in the crypt. The medals he had struck and coinage he had minted would be buried with him to identify him to anyone who might dig him up a thousand years later. They would seal him in three coffins — one of cypress; one of lead to keep him from the damp and to carry his coat of arms, and the certificate of his death; the last of elm so that he might seem, at least, like other men who go to the grave in a wooden box.

The Pope was dead. So they would pray for him as for any other: 'Enter not into judgement with thy servant, O Lord . . . Deliver him from eternal death.' Then they would lower him into the vault under the High Altar, where perhaps — but only perhaps — he would moulder into dust with the dust of Peter; and a mason would brick up the vault and fix on a marble tablet with his name, his title and the date of his birth and his obit.

The Pope was dead. They would mourn him with nine days of masses and give him nine absolutions — of which, having been greater in his life than other men, he might have greater need after his death.

Then they would forget him, because the See of Peter was vacant, the life of the Church was in syncope and the Almighty was without a vicar on this troubled planet.

The See of Peter was vacant. So the cardinals of the Sacred College assumed trusteeship over the authority of the Fisherman, though they lacked the power to exercise it. The power did not reside in them but in Christ and none could assume it but by lawful transmission and election.

The See of Peter was vacant. So they struck two medals, one for the Camerlengo, which bore a large umbrella over crossed keys. There was no-one under the umbrella, and this was a sign to the most ignorant that there was no incumbent for the Chair of the Apostles, and that all that was done had only an interim character. The second medal was that of the Governor of the Conclave: he who must assemble the cardinals of the Church, and lock them inside the chambers of the conclave and keep them there until they had issued with a new Pope.

Every coin new-minted in the Vatican City, every stamp now issued, bore the words *sede vacante*, which even those without Latinity might understand as 'while the Chair is vacant'. The Vatican newspaper carried the same sign on its front page, and would wear a black band of mourning until the new Pontiff was named.

Every news service in the world had a representative camped on the doorstep of the Vatican press office; and from each point of the compass old men came, bent with years of infirmity, to put on the scarlet of princes and sit in conclave for the making of a new Pope.

There were Carlin the American, and Rahamani the Syrian, and Hsien the Chinese, and Hanna the Irishman from Australia. There were Councha from Brazil, and da Costa from Portugal. There were Morand from Paris, and Lavigne from Brussels, and Lambertini from Venice, and Brandon from London. There were a Pole and two Germans, and a Ukrainian who nobody knew because his name had been reserved in the breast of the last Pope and had been proclaimed only a few days before his death. In all there were eighty-five men, of whom the eldest was ninety-two and the youngest, the Ukrainian, was fifty. As each of them arrived in the city, he presented himself and his credentials to the urbane and gentle Valerio Rinaldi, who was the Cardinal Camerlengo.

Rinaldi welcomed each with a slim, dry hand and a smile of mild irony. To each he administered the oath of the conclavist: that he understood and would rigorously observe all the rules of the election as laid down in the Apostolic Constitution of 1945, that he would under pain of a reserved excommunication preserve the secret of the election, that he would not serve by his votes the interest of any secular power, that, if he were elected Pope, he would not surrender any temporal right of the Holy See which might be deemed necessary for its independence.

No-one refused the oath; but Rinaldi, who had a sense of humour, wondered many times why it was necessary to administer it at all — unless the Church had a healthy disrespect for the virtues of its princes. Old men were apt to be too easily wounded. So, when he outlined the terms of the oath, Valerio Rinaldi laid a mild emphasis on the counsel of the Apostolic Constitution, that all the proceedings of the election should be conducted with 'prudence, charity, and a singular calm'.

His caution was not unjustified. The history of papal elections was a stormy one, at times downright turbulent. When Damasus the Spaniard was elected in the fourth century, there were massacres in the churches of the city. Leo V was imprisoned, tortured and murdered by the Theophylacts, so that for nearly a century the Church was ruled by puppets directed by the Theophylact women, Theodora and Marozia. In the conclave of 1623 eight cardinals and forty of their assistants died of malaria, and there were harsh scenes and rough words over the election of the Saint, Pius X.

All in all, Rinaldi concluded — though he was wise enough to keep the conclusion to himself — it was best not to trust too much to the crusty tempers and the frustrated vanities of old men. Which brought him by a round turn to the problem of housing and feeding eighty-five of them with their servants and assistants until the election should be finished. Some of them, it seemed, would have to take over quarters from the Swiss Guard. None of them could be lodged too far from bathroom or toilet, and all had to be provided with a minimum service by way of cooks, barbers, surgeons, physicians, valets, porters, secretaries, waiters, carpenters, plumbers, firemen (in case any weary prelate nodded off with a cigar in his hand!). If (God forbid!) any cardinal were in prison or under indictment, he had to be brought to the conclave and made to perform his functions under military guard.

This time, however, no-one was in prison — except Krizanic in Yugoslavia, and he was in prison for the faith, which was a different matter — and the late Pope had run an efficient administration, so that Valerio Cardinal Rinaldi even had time to spare to meet with his colleague, Leone of the Holy Office, who was also the Dean of the Sacred College. Leone lived up to his name. He had a grey lion's mane and a growling temper. He was, moreover, a Roman, bred-in-the-bone, dyed-in-the-wool. Rome was for him the centre of the world, and central-ism was a doctrine almost as immutable as that of the Trinity and the Procession of the Holy Ghost. With his great eagle beak and his jowly jaw, he looked like a senator strayed out of Augustan times, and his pale eyes looked out on the world with wintry disapproval.

Innovation was for him the first step toward heresy, and he sat in the Holy Office like a grizzled watchdog, whose hackles would rise at the first unfamiliar sound in doctrine interpretation, or practice. One of his French colleagues had said, with more wit than charity, 'Leone smells of the fire.' But the general belief was that he would plunge his own hand into the flame rather than set his signature to the smallest deviation from orthodoxy.

Rinaldi respected him, though he had never been able to like him, and so their intercourse had been limited to the courtesies of their common trade. Tonight, however, the old lion seemed in a gentler mood, and was disposed to be talkative. His pale, watchful eyes were lit with a momentary amusement.

'I'm eighty-two, my friend, and I've buried three Popes. I'm beginning to feel lonely.'

'If we don't get a younger man this time,' said Rinaldi mildly, 'you may well bury a fourth.'

Leone shot him a quick look from under his shaggy brows. 'And what's that supposed to mean?'

Rinaldi shrugged, and spread his fine hands in a Roman gesture. 'Just what it says. We're all too old. There are not more than half-a-dozen of us who can give the Church what it needs at this moment: personality, a decisive policy, time and continuity to make the policy work.'

'Do you think you're one of the half-dozen?'

Rinaldi smiled with thin irony. 'I know I'm not. When the new man is chosen — whoever he is — I propose to offer him my resignation, and ask his permission to rusticate at home. It's taken me fifteen years to build a garden in that place of mine. I'd like a little while to enjoy it.'

'Do you think I have a chance of election?' asked Leone bluntly.

'I hope not,' said Rinaldi.

Leone threw back his great mane and laughed. 'Don't worry. I know I haven't. They need someone quite different; someone —' he hesitated, fumbling for the phrase — 'someone who has compassion on the multitude, who sees them, as Christ saw them — sheep without a shepherd. I'm not that sort of man. I wish I were.'

Leone heaved his bulky body out of the chair, and walked to the big table where an antique globe stood among a litter of books. He spun the globe slowly on its axis so that now one country, now another, swam into the light. 'Look at it, my friend! The world, our vineyard! Once we colonised it in the name of Christ. Not righteously always, not always justly or wisely, but the cross was there, and the sacraments were there, and however a man lived — in purple or in chains — there was a chance for him to die like a son of God. Now . . . ? Now we are everywhere in retreat. China is lost to us, and Asia and all the Russias. Africa will soon be gone, and the South Americas will be next. You know it. I know it. It is the measure of our failure that we have sat all these years in Rome, and watched it happen.' He checked the spinning globe with an unsteady hand, and then turned to face his visitor, with a new question. 'If you had your life over, Rinaldi, what would you do with it?'

Rinaldi looked up with that deprecating smile which lent him so much charm. 'I think I should probably do the same things again. Not that I'm very proud of them, but they happened to be the only things I could do well. I get along with people, because I've never been capable of very deep feelings about them. That makes me, I suppose, a natural diplomat. I don't like to quarrel. I like even less to be emotionally involved. I like privacy and I enjoy study. So I'm a good canonist, a reasonable historian, and an adequate linguist. I've never had very strong passions. You might, if you felt malicious, call me a cold fish. So I've achieved a reputation for good conduct without having to work for it . . . All in all, I've had a very satisfactory life — satisfactory to myself, of course. How the recording angel sees it, is another matter.'

'Don't underrate yourself, man,' said Leone sourly. 'You've done a great deal better than you'll admit.'

'I need time and reflection to set my soul in order,' said Rinaldi quietly. 'May I count on you to help me resign?'

'Of course.'

'Thank you. Now, suppose the inquisitor answers his own question. What would you do if you had to begin again?'

'I've thought about it often,' said Leone heavily. 'If I didn't marry — and I'm not sure but that's what I needed to make me halfway human — I'd be a country priest with just enough theology to hear confession, and just enough Latin to get through mass and the sacramental formulae. But with heart enough to know what griped in the guts of other men, and made them cry into their pillows at night. I'd sit in front of my church on a summer evening and read my office and talk about the weather and the crops, and learn to be gentle with the poor and humble with the unhappy ones . . . You know what I am now? A walking encyclopaedia of dogma and theological controversy. I can smell out an error faster than a Dominican. And what does it mean? Nothing. Who cares about theology except the theologians? We are necessary but less important than we think. The Church is Christ — Christ and the people. And all the people want to know is whether or no there is a God, and what is His relation with them, and how they can get back to Him when they stray.'

'Large questions,' said Rinaldi gently, 'not to be answered by small minds or gross ones.'

Leone shook his lion's mane stubbornly. 'For the people they come down to simplicities. Why shouldn't I covet my neighbour's wife? Who takes the revenge that is forbidden to me? And who cares when I am sick and tired, and dying in an upstairs room? I can give them a theologian's answer. But whom do they believe but the man who feels the answers in his heart, and bears the scars of their consequences in his own flesh? Where are the men like that? Is there one among all of us who wear the red hat? Eh . . . !' His grim mouth twitched into a grin of embarrassment, and he flung out his arms in mock despair. 'We are what we are, and God has to take half the responsibility even for theologians! . . . Now tell me — where do we go for our Pope?'

'This time,' said Rinaldi crisply, 'we should choose him for the people and not for ourselves.'

'There will be eighty-five of us in the conclave. How many will agree on what is best for the people?'

Rinaldi looked down at the backs of his carefully manicured fingers. He said softly, 'If we showed them the man first, perhaps we could get them to agree.'

Leone's answer was swift and emphatic. 'You would have to show him to me first.'

'And if you agreed?'

'Then there would be another question,' said Leone flatly. 'How many of our brethren will think as we do?'

The question was subtler than it looked, and they both knew it. Here, in fact, was the whole loaded issue of a papal election, the whole paradox of the Papacy. The man who wore the Fisherman's ring was Vicar of Christ, Vicegerent of the Almighty. His dominion was spiritual and universal. He was the servant of all the servants of God, even of those who did not acknowledge him.

On the other hand, he was Bishop of Rome, Metropolitan of an Italian see. The Romans claimed by historic tradition a pre-emption on his presence and his services. They relied on him for employment, for the tourist trade and the bolstering of their economy by Vatican investment, for the preservation of their historic monuments and national privileges. His court was Italian in character; the greater number of his household and his administrators were Italian. If he could not deal with them familiarly in their own tongue, he stood naked to palace intrigue and every kind of partisan interest.

Once upon a time the Roman view had had a peculiarly universal aspect. The numen of the ancient empire still hung about it, and the memory of the Pax Romana had not yet vanished from the consciousness of Europe. But the numen was fading. Imperial Rome had never subdued Russia or Asia, and the Latins who conquered South America had brought no peace, but the sword. England had revolted long since, as she had revolted earlier from the legions of Roman occupation. So that there was sound argument for a new, non-Italian succession to the papal throne — just as there was sound reason for believing that a non-Italian might become either a puppet of his ministers or a victim of their talent for intrigue.

The perpetuity of the Church was an article of faith; but its diminutions and corruptions, and its jeopardy by the follies of its members, were part of the canon of history. There was plenty of ground for cynicism. But over and over again the cynics were confounded by the uncanny capacity for self-renewal in the Church and in the Papacy. The cynics had their own explanations. The faithful put it down to the indwelling of the Holy Ghost. Either way there was an uncomfortable mystery: how the chaos of history could issue in so consistent a hold on dogma or why an omniscient God chose such a messy method of preserving His foothold in the minds of His creatures.

So every conclave began with the invocation of the Paraclete. On the day of the walling-in, Rinaldi led his old men and their attendants into St Peter's. Then Leone came, dressed in a scarlet chasuble and accompanied by his deacons and subdeacons, to begin the Mass of the Holy Spirit. As he watched the celebrant, weighed down by the elaborate vestments, moving painfully through the ritual of the sacrifice, Rinaldi felt a pang of pity for him and a sudden rush of understanding.

They were all in the same galley, these leaders of the Church — himself along with them. They were men without issue, who had 'made themselves eunuchs for the love of God'. A long time since they had dedicated themselves with greater or less sincerity to the service of a hidden God, and to the propagation of an unprovable mystery. Through the temporality of the Church they had attained to honour, more honour perhaps than any of them might have attained in the secular state, but they all lay under the common burden of age — failing faculties, the loneliness of eminence, and the fear of a reckoning that might find them bankrupt debtors.

He thought, too, of the stratagem which he had planned with Leone, to introduce a candidate who was still a stranger to most of the voters, and to promote his cause without breaching the Apostolic Constitution which they had sworn to preserve. He wondered if this were not a presumption and an attempt to circumvent Providence, whom they were invoking at this very moment. Yet, if God had chosen, as the faith taught, to use man as a free instrument for a divine plan, how else could one act? One could not let so momentous an occasion as a papal election play itself like a game of chance. Prudence was enjoined on all — prayerful preparation and then considered action, and afterwards resignation and submission. Yet however prudently one planned, one could not escape the uncanny feeling that one walked unwary and unpurged on sacred ground.

The heat, the flicker of the candles, the chant of the choir, and the mesmeric pace of the ritual made him drowsy, and he stole a surreptitious glance at his colleagues to see if any of them had noticed his nodding.

Like twin choirs of ancient archangels they sat on either side of the sanctuary, their breasts hung with golden crosses, the princely seals agleam on their folded hands, their faces scored by age and the experience of power.

There was Rahamani of Antioch, with his spade beard and his craggy brows and his bright, half-mystical eyes. There was Benedetti, round as a dumpling with pink cheeks and candyfloss hair, who ran the Vatican Bank. Next to him was Potocki from Poland, he of the high, bald dome and the suffering mouth and the wise, calculating eyes. Tatsue from Japan wanted only the saffron robe to make him a Buddhist image, and Hsien, the exiled Chinese, sat between Ragambwe, the black man from Kenya, and Pallenberg, the lean ascetic from Munich.

Rinaldi's shrewd eyes ranged along the choir stalls, naming each one for his virtues or his shortcomings, trying on each the classic label *papabile*, he-who-has-the-makings-of-a-Pope. In theory every member of the conclave could wear it; in practice very few were eligible.

Age was a bar to some. Talent or temperament or reputation was an impediment to others. Nationality was a vital question. One could not elect an American without seeming to divide East and West even further. A Negro Pope might seem a spectacular symbol of the new revolutionary nations, just as a Japanese might be a useful link between Asia and Europe. But the princes of the Church were old men and as wary of spectacular gestures as they were of historic hangovers. A German Pope might alienate the sympathies of those who had suffered in World War II. A Frenchman would recall old memories of Avignon and tramontane rebellions. While there were still dictatorships in Spain and Portugal, an Iberian Pope could be a diplomatic indiscretion. Gonfalone, the Milanese, had the reputation of being a saint, but he was becoming more and more of a recluse, and there was question of his fitness for so public an office. Leone was an autocrat who might well mistake the fire of zealotry for the flame of compassion.

The lector was reading from the Acts of the Apostles. 'In those days, Peter began and said, Men, Brethren, the Lord charged us to preach to the people and to testify that He is the one who has been appointed by God to be judge of the living and of the dead. . . .' The choir sang, '*Veni, Sancte Spiritus* . . . Come Holy Spirit and fill the hearts of your faithful ones . . .' Then Leone began to read in his strong stubborn voice the gospel for the day of the conclave: 'He who enters not by the door into the sheepfold, but climbs up another way is a thief and a robber. But he who enters by the door is the shepherd of the sheep.' Rinaldi bent his head in his hands and prayed that the man he was offering would be in truth a shepherd, and that the conclave might hand him the crook and the ring.

When the Mass was over, the celebrant retired to the sacristy to take off his vestments, and the cardinals relaxed in the stalls. Some of them whispered to one another, a couple were still nodding drowsily, and one was seen to take a surreptitious pinch of snuff. The next part of the ceremony was a formality, but it promised to be a boring one. A prelate would read them a homily in Latin, pointing out once again the importance of the election and their moral obligation to carry it out in an orderly and honest fashion. By ancient custom, the prelate was chosen for the purity of his Latin, but this time the Camerlengo had made another arrangement.

A whisper of surprise stirred round the assembly as they saw Rinaldi leave his place and walk down to the far end of the stalls on the gospel side of the altar. He offered his hand to a tall, thin cardinal and led him to the pulpit. When he stood elevated in the full glare of the lights, they saw that he was the youngest of them all. His hair was black, his square beard was black too, and down his left cheek was a long, livid scar. On his breast, in addition to the cross, was a pectoral ikon representing a Byzantine Madonna and Child. When he crossed himself, he made the sign from right to left in the Slavonic manner; yet, when he began in speak, it was not in Latin but in a pure and melodious Tuscan. Across the nave Leone smiled a grim approval at Rinaldi, and then they surrendered themselves like their colleagues to the simple eloquence of the stranger.

'My name is Kiril Lakota, and I am come the latest and the least into this Sacred College. I speak to you today by the invitation of our brother the Cardinal Camerlengo. To most of you I am a stranger because my people are scattered, and I have spent the last seventeen years in prison. If I have any rights among you, any credit at all, let this be the foundation of them — that I speak for the lost ones, for those who walk in darkness and in the valley of the shadow of death. It is for them and not for ourselves that we are entering into conclave. It is for them and not for ourselves that we must elect a Pontiff. The first man who held this office was one who walked with Christ, and was crucified like the Master. Those who have best served the Church and the faithful are those who have been closest to Christ and to the people, who are the image of Christ. We have power in our hands, my brothers. We shall put even greater power into the hands of the man we elect; but we must use the power as servants and not as masters. We must consider that we are what we are — priests, bishops, pastors — by virtue of an act of dedication to the people who are the flock of Christ. What we possess, even to the clothes on our backs, comes to us out of their charity. The whole material fabric of the Church was raised stone on stone, gold on golden offering, by the sweat of the faithful, and they have given it into our hands for stewardship. It is they who have educated us so that we may teach them and their children. It is they who humble themselves before our priesthood, as before the divine priesthood of Christ. It is for them that we exercise the sacramental and the sacrificial powers which are given to us in the anointing and the laying-on of hands. If in our deliberations we serve any other cause but this, then we are traitors. It is not asked of us that we shall agree on what is best for the Church, but only that we shall deliberate in charity and humility, and in the end give our obedience to the man who shall be chosen by the majority. We are asked to act swiftly so that the Church may not be left without a head. In all this we must be what, in the end, our Pontiff shall proclaim himself to be — servants of the servants of God. Let us in these final moments resign ourselves as willing instruments for His hands. Amen.'

It was so simply said that it might have been the customary formality, yet the man himself, with his scarred face and his strong voice and his crooked, eloquent hands, lent to the words an unexpected poignancy. There was a long silence while he left the pulpit and returned to his own place. Leone nodded his lion's head in approval, and Rinaldi breathed a silent prayer of gratitude. Then the master of ceremonies took command and led the cardinals and their attendants with their confessor and their physician and surgeon, and the architect of the conclave, and the conclave workmen out of the Basilica and into the confines of the Vatican itself.

In the Sistine Chapel they were sworn again. Then Leone gave the order for the bells to be rung, so that all who did not belong to the conclave should leave the sealed area at once. The servants led each of the cardinals to his apartment. Then the prefect of the master of ceremonies, with the architect of the conclave, began the ritual search of the enclosed area. They went from room to room pulling aside draperies, throwing light into dark corners, opening closets, until every space was declared free from intruders.

At the entrance of the great stairway of Pius IX they halted and the noble guard marched out of the conclave area, followed by the marshal of the conclave and his aides. The great door was locked. The marshal of the conclave turned his key on the outside. On the inside the masters of ceremonies turned their own key. The marshal ordered his flag hoisted over the Vatican, and from this moment no-one might leave or enter, or pass a message, until the new Pope was elected and named.

———•———

Alone in his quarters, Kiril Cardinal Lakota was beginning a private purgatory. It was a recurrent state whose symptoms were now familiar to him: a cold sweat that broke out on face and palms, a trembling in the limbs, a twitching of the severed nerves in his face, a panic fear that the room was closing in to crush him. Twice in his life he had been walled up in the bunkers of an underground prison. Four months in all, he had endured the terrors of darkness and cold and solitude and near starvation, so that the pillars of his reason had rocked under the strain. Nothing in his years of Siberian exile had afflicted him so much, nor left so deep a scar on his memory. Nothing had brought him so close to abjuration and apostasy.

He had been beaten often, but the bruised tissue had healed itself in time. He had been interrogated till every nerve was screaming and his mind had lapsed into a merciful confusion. From this too he had emerged, stronger in faith and in reason, but the horror of solitary confinement would remain with him until he died. Kamenev had kept his promise. 'You will never be able to forget me. Wherever you go, I shall be. Whatever you become, I shall be part of you.' Even here, in the neutral confines of the Vatican City, in the princely room under

Raphael's frescoes, Kamenev, the insidious tormentor, was with him. There was only one escape from him, and that was the one he had learned in the bunker — the projection of the tormented spirit into the arms of the Almighty.

He threw himself on his knees, buried his face in his hands, and tried to concentrate every faculty of mind and body into the simple act of abandonment.

His lips commanded no words, but the will seized on the plaint of Christ in Gethsemane. 'Father, if it be possible, let this Chalice pass.'

In the end he knew it would pass, but first the agony must be endured. The walls pressed in upon him relentlessly. The ceiling weighed down on him like a leaden vestment. The darkness pressed upon his eyeballs and packed itself inside his skull-case. Every muscle in his body knotted in pain and his teeth chattered as if from the rigours of fever. Then he became deathly cold, and deathly calm, and waited passively for the light that was the beginning of peace and of communion.

The light was like a dawn seen from a high hill, flooding swiftly into every fold of the landscape, so that the whole pattern of its history was revealed at one glance. The road of his own pilgrimage was there like a scarlet ribbon that stretched four thousand miles from Lvov, in the Ukraine, to Nokolayevsk on the sea of Okhotsk.

When the war with the Germans was over, he had been named, in spite of his youth, Metropolitan of Lvov, successor to the great and saintly Andrew Szepticky, leader of all the Ruthenian Catholics. Shortly afterwards he had been arrested with six other bishops and deported to the eastern limits of Siberia. The six others had died, and he had been left alone, shepherd of a lost flock, to carry the cross on his own shoulders.

For seventeen years he had been in prison, or in the labour camps. Once only in all that time he had been able to say mass, with a thimbleful of wine and a crust of white bread. All that he could cling to of doctrine and prayer and sacramental formulae was locked in his own brain. All that he had tried to spend of strength and compassion upon his fellow prisoners, he had had to dredge out of himself and out of the well of the divine mercy. Yet his body, weakened by torture, had grown miraculously strong again at slave labour in the mines and on the road gangs, so that even Kamenev could no longer mock him, but was struck with wonder at his survival.

For Kamenev, his tormentor in the first interrogations, would always come back; and each time he came, he had risen a little higher in the Marxist order. Each time he had seemed a little more friendly as if he were making a slow surrender to respect for his victim.

Even from the mountain-top of contemplation, he could still see Kamenev cold, sardonic, searching him for the slightest sign of weakness, the slightest hint of surrender. In the beginning he had had to force himself to pray for the jailer. After a while they had come to a bleak kind of brotherhood, even as the one rose higher and the other seemed to sink deeper into a fellowship with the Siberian slaves. In the end, it was Kamenev who had organised his escape — inflicting on him a final irony by giving him the identity of a dead man.

'You will go free,' Kamenev had said, 'because I need you free. But you will always owe me a debt because I have killed a man to give you a name. One day, I shall come to you to ask for payment, and you will pay, whatever it may cost.'

It was as though the jailer had assumed the mantle of prophecy, because Kiril Lakota had escaped and made his way to Rome to find that a dying Pope had made him a cardinal 'in the breast' — a man of destiny, a hinge-man of Mother Church.

To this point the road in retrospect was clear. He could trace in its tragedies the promise of future mercies. For every one of the bishops who had died for his belief, a man had died in his arms in the camp, blessing the Almighty for a final absolution. The scattered flock would not all lose the faith for which they had suffered. Some of them would remain to hand on the creed, and to keep a small light burning that one day might light a thousand torches. In the degradation of the road gangs, he had seen how the strangest men upheld the human dignities. He had baptised children with a handful of dirty water and seen them die unmarked by the miseries of the world.

He himself had learned humility and gratitude and the courage to believe in an omnipotence working by a mighty evolution toward an ultimate good. He had learned compassion and tenderness and the meaning of the cry in the night. He had learned to hope that for Kamenev himself he might be an instrument, if not of ultimate enlightenment, then at least of ultimate absolution. But all this was in the past, and the pattern had still to work itself out beyond Rome into a fathomless future. Even the light of contemplation was not thrown beyond Rome. There was a veil drawn, and the veil was the limit imposed on prescience by a merciful God . . .

The light was changing now; the landscape of the steppes had become an undulant sea, across which a figure in antique robes was walking toward him, his face shining, his pierced hands outstretched, as if in greeting. Kiril Cardinal Lakota shrank away, and tried to bury himself in the lighted sea; but there was no escape. When the hands touched him and the luminous face bent to embrace him, he felt himself pierced by an intolerable joy, and an intolerable pain. Then he entered into the moment of peace.

The servant who was assigned to care for him came into the room and saw him kneeling rigid as a cataleptic with his arms outstretched in the attitude of crucifixion. Rinaldi, making the rounds of the conclavists, came upon him and tried vainly to wake him. Then Rinaldi too went away, shaken and humbled, to consult with Leone and his colleagues.

In his cluttered and unelegant office, George Faber, the grey-haired dean of the Roman press corps, fifteen years Italian correspondent for the New York *Monitor*, was writing his background story on the papal election:

'. . . Outside the small medieval enclave of the Vatican, the world is in a climate of crisis. Winds of change are blowing and storm warnings are being raised, now in one place, now in another. The arms race between America and Russia goes on unabated. Every month there are new and hostile probes into the high orbits of space. There is famine in India, and guerrilla fighting along the southern peninsulas of Asia. There is thunder over Africa, and the tattered flags of revolution are being hoisted over the capitals of South America. There is blood on the sands in North Africa, and in Europe the battle for economic survival is waged behind the closed doors of banks and board rooms. In the high airs above the Pacific, war planes fly to sample the pollution of the air by lethal atomic particles. In China the new dynasts struggle to fill the bellies of hungry millions, while they hold their minds chained to the rigid orthodoxy of Marxist philosophy. In the misty valleys of the Himalayas, where the prayer-flags flutter and the tea-pickers plod along the terraces, there are forays and incursions from Tibet and Sinkiang. On the frontiers of Outer Mongolia, the uneasy amity of Russia and China is strained to the point of rupture. Patrol boats probe the mangrove swamps and inlets of New Guinea, while the upland tribes try to project themselves into the twentieth century by a single leap from the Stone Age.

'Everywhere man has become aware of himself as a transient animal and is battling desperately to assert his right to the best of the world for the short time that he sojourns in it. The Nepalese haunted by his mountain demons, the coolie hauling his heart muscle into exhaustion between the shafts of a rickshaw, the Israeli beleaguered at every frontier, everyone all at once is asserting his claim to an identity; everyone has an ear for any prophet who can promise him one.'

He stopped typing, lit a cigarette and leaned back in his chair, considering the thought which he had just written — 'a claim to identity'. Strange how everyone had to make it sooner or later. Strange for how long one accepted with apparent equanimity the kind of person one seemed to be, the state to which one had apparently been nominated in life. Then all of a sudden, the identity was called in question . . . His own for instance. George Faber, long-time bachelor, acknowledged expert on Italian affairs and Vatican politics. Why so late in life was he being forced to question what he was, what he had so far been content to be? Why this relentless dissatisfaction with the public image of himself? Why this doubt that he could survive any longer without a permanent supplement to himself? . . . A woman, of course. There always had been women in his life, but Chiara was something new and special . . . The thought often troubled him. He tried to put it away and bent again to his typewriter:

'Everywhere the cry is for survival, but since the supreme irony of creation was that man must inevitably die, those who strived for the mastery of his mind or his muscle have to promise him an extension of his span into some semblance of immortality. The Marxist promises him a oneness with the workers of the world. The Nationalist gives him a flag and a frontier, and a local enlargement of himself. The Democrat offers him liberty through a ballot box, but warns that he might have to die to preserve it.

'But for man, and all the prophets he raises up for himself, the last enemy is time; and time is a relative dimension, limited directly by man's capacity to make use of it. Modern communication, swift as light, has diminished to nothing the time between a human act and its consequences. A shot fired in Berlin can detonate the world within minutes. A plague in the Philippines can infect Australia within a day. A man toppling from a high wire in a Moscow circus can be watched in his death agony from London and New York.

'So, at every moment, every man is besieged by the consequences of his own sins and those of all his fellows. So, too, every prophet and every pundit is haunted by the swift lapse of time and the knowledge that the accounting for false predictions and broken promises is swifter than it has ever been in history. Here precisely is the cause of the crisis. Here the winds and the waves are born and the thunderbolts are forged that may, any week, any month, go roaring round the world under a sky black with mushroom clouds.

'The men in the Vatican are aware of time, though many of them have ceased to be as aware as they need to be. . . .'

Time . . . ! He had become so vividly conscious of this diminishing dimension of existence. He was in his mid-forties. For more than a year he had been trying to steer Chiara's petition of nullity through the Holy Roman Rota so that she might be free from Corrado Calitri to marry him. But the case was moving with desperate slowness, and Faber, although a Catholic by birth, had come to resent bitterly the impersonal system of the Roman congregations and the attitude of the old men who ran them.

He typed on vividly, precisely, professionally:

'Like most old men they are accustomed to seeing time as a flash between two eternities instead of a quantum of extension given to each individual man to mature toward the vision of his God.

'They are concerned also with man's identity, which they are obliged to affirm as the identity of a son of God. Yet here they are in danger of another pitfall: that they sometimes affirm his identity without understanding his individuality, and how he has to grow in whatever garden he is planted, whether the ground is sweet or sour, whether the air is friendly or tempestuous. Men grow, like trees, in different shapes, crooked or straight, according to the climate of their nurture. But so long as the sap flows and the leaves burgeon, there should be no quarrel with the shape of the man or the tree.

'The men of the Vatican are concerned as well with immortality and eternity. They too understand man's need for an extension of himself beyond the limit of the fleeting years. They affirm, as of faith, the persistence of soul into an eternity of union with the Creator, or of exile from His face. They go further. They promise man a preservation of his identity and an ultimate victory even over the terror of physical death. What they fail too often to understand is that immortality must be begun in time, and that a man must be given the physical resources to survive before his spirit can grow to desire more than physical survival. . . .'

Chiara had become as necessary to him as breath. Without her youth and her passion, it seemed that he must slide all too quickly into age and disillusion. She had been his mistress for nearly six months now, but he was plagued by the fear that he could lose her at any moment to a younger man, and that the promise of children and continuity might never be fulfilled in him . . . He had friends in the Vatican. He had easy access to men with great names in the Church, but they were committed to the law and to the system, and they could not help him at all. He wrote feelingly:

'They are caught, these old and deliberate men, in the dilemma of all principality: that the higher one rises, the more one sees of the world, but the less one apprehends of the small determining factors of human existence. How a man without shoes may starve because he cannot walk to a place of employment. How a liverish tax collector may start a local revolution. How high blood pressure may plunge a noble man into melancholy and despair. How a woman may sell herself for money because she cannot give herself to one man for love. The danger of all rulers is that they begin to believe that history is the result of great generalities, instead of the sum of millions of small particulars, like bad drainage and sexual obsession and the anopheles mosquito . . .'

It was not the story he had intended to write, but it was a true record of his personal feelings about the coming event . . . Let it stand then! Let the editors in New York like it or lump it . . . ! The door opened and Chiara came in. He took her in his arms and kissed her. He damned the Church and her husband and his paper to a special kind of hell, and then took her out to lunch on the Via Veneto.

The first day of the conclave was left private to the electing cardinals, so that they might meet and talk discreetly, and probe for one another's prejudices and blind spots and motives of private interest. It was for this reason that Rinaldi and Leone moved among them to prepare them carefully for the final proposal. Once the voting began, once they had taken sides with this candidate or that, it would be much more difficult to bring them to an agreement.

Not all the talk was on the level of eternal verities. Much of it was simple and blunt, like Rinaldi's conversation with the American over a cup of American coffee (brewed by His Eminence's own servant because Italian coffee gave him indigestion).

His Eminence, Charles Corbet Carlin, Cardinal Archbishop of New York, was a tall, ruddy man with an expansive manner and a shrewd, pragmatic eye. He stated his problem as baldly as a banker challenging an overdraft:

'We don't want a diplomat, and we don't want a Curia official who will look at the world through a Roman eyeglass. A man who has travelled, yes, but someone who has been a pastor and understands what our problems are at this moment.'

'I should be interested to hear Your Eminence define them.' Rinaldi was at his most urbane.

'We're losing our grip on the people,' said Carlin flatly. 'They are losing their loyalty to us. I think we are more than half to blame.'

Rinaldi was startled. Carlin had the reputation of being a brilliant banker for Mother Church and of entertaining a conviction that all the ills of the world could be solved by a well-endowed school system and a rousing sermon every Sunday. To hear him talk so bluntly of the shortcomings of his own province was both refreshing and disquieting. Rinaldi asked:

'Why are we losing our grip?'

'In America? Two reasons: prosperity and respectability. We're not persecuted anymore. We pay our way. We can wear the faith like a Rotary badge — and with as little social consequence. We collect our dues like a club, shout down the communists, and make the biggest contribution in the whole world to Peter's Pence. But it isn't enough. There's no — no heart in it for many Catholics. The young ones are drifting outside our influence. The don't need us as they should. They don't trust us as they used. For that,' he added gravely, 'I think I'm partly to blame.'

'None of us has much right to be proud of himself,' said Rinaldi quietly. 'Look at France — look at the bloody things that have been done in Algeria. Yet this is a country half-Catholic, and with a Catholic leadership. Where is our authority in this monstrous situation? A third of the Catholic population of the world is in the South Americas, yet what is our influence there?

What impression do we make among the indifferent rich, and the oppressed poor, who see no hope in God and less in those who represent Him? Where do we begin to change?'

'I've made mistakes,' said Carlin moodily. 'Big ones. I can't even begin to repair them all. My father was a gardener, a good one. He used to say that the best you could do for a tree was mulch it and prune it once a year, and leave the rest to God. I always prided myself that I was a practical fellow like he was — you know? Build the Church, then the school. Get the nuns in, then the brothers. Build the seminary and train the priests, and keep the money coming in. After that it was up to the Almighty.' For the first time he smiled, and Rinaldi, who had disliked him for many years, began to warm to him. He went on whimsically, 'The Romans and the Irish! We're great plotters, and great builders, but we lose the inwardness of things quicker than anybody else. Stick to the book! No meat on Fridays, no sleeping with your neighbour's wife, and leave the mysteries to the theologians! It isn't enough. God help us, but it isn't!'

'You're asking for a saint. I doubt we have many on the books just now.'

'Not a saint.' Carlin was emphatic again. 'A man for the people, and of the people, like Sarto was. A man who could bleed for them, and scold them, and have them know all the time that he loved them. A man who could break out of this gilded garden patch and make himself another Peter.'

'He would be crucified too, of course,' said Rinaldi tartly.

'Perhaps that is just what we need,' said His Eminence from New York.

Whereupon Rinaldi, the diplomat, judged it opportune to talk of the bearded Ukrainian, Kiril Lakota, as a-man-with-the-makings-of-a-Pope.

———•———

In a somewhat smaller suite of the conclave, Leone was discussing the same candidate with Hugh Cardinal Brandon from Westminster. Brandon, being English, was a man with no illusions and few enthusiasms. He pursed his thin, grey lips and toyed with his pectoral cross, and delivered his policy in precise, if stilted Italian:

'From our point of view, an Italian is still the best choice. It leaves us room to move, if you understand what I mean. There is no question of a new attitude or a fresh political alignment. There is no disturbance of the relations between the Vatican and the Republic of Italy. The Papacy would still be an effective barrier to any growth of Italian communism.' He permitted himself a dry joke. 'We could still count on the sympathy of English romantics for romantic Italy.'

Leone, veteran of many a subtle argument, nodded his agreement and added almost casually, 'You would not then consider our newcomer, the one who spoke to us this morning?'

'I doubt it. I found him, as everyone did, most impressive in the pulpit. But then eloquence is hardly a full qualification, is it? Besides, there is the question of rites. I understand this man is a Ukrainian and belongs to the Ruthenian rite.'

'If he were elected, he would automatically practise the Roman one.'

His Eminence of Westminster smiled thinly. 'The beard might worry some people. A too Byzantine look, don't you think? We haven't had a bearded Pope in a very long time.'

'No doubt he would shave it.'

'Would he still wear the ikon?'

'He might be persuaded to dispense with that, too.'

'Then we should be left with a model Roman. So why not choose an Italian in the first place? I can't believe you would want anything different.'

'Believe me, I do. I am prepared to tell you now that my vote will go to the Ukrainian.'

'I am afraid I can't promise you mine. The English and the Russians, you know . . . Historically we've never done very well together . . . Never at all.'

———•———

'Always,' said Rahamani the Syrian in his pliant, courteous fashion, 'always you search a man for the one necessary gift — the gift of cooperation with God. Even among good men this gift is rare. Most of us, you see, spend our lives trying to bend ourselves to the will of God, and even then we have often to be bent by a violent grace. The others, the rare ones, commit themselves, as if by an instinctive act, to be tools in the hands of the Maker. If this new man is such a one, then it is he whom we need.'

'And how do we know?' asked Leone dryly.

'We submit him to God,' said the Syrian. 'We ask God to judge him, and we rest secure in the outcome.'

'We can only vote on him. There is no other way.'

'There is another way, prescribed in the Apostolic Constitution. It is the way of inspiration. Any member of the conclave may make a public proclamation of the man he believes should be chosen, trusting that if this be a candidate acceptable to God, God will inspire the other conclavists to approve him publicly. It is a valid method of election.'

'It also takes courage — and a great deal of faith.'

'If we elders of the Church lack faith, what hope is there for the people?'

'I am reproved,' said the Cardinal Secretary of the Holy Office. 'It's time I stopped canvassing and began to pray.'

Early the next morning, all the cardinals assembled in the Sistine Chapel for the first ballot. For each there was a throne and over the throne a silken canopy. The thrones were arranged along the walls of the Chapel, and before each was set a small table, which bore the cardinal's coat of arms and his name inscribed in Latin. The chapel altar was covered with a tapestry upon which was embroidered a figuration of the Holy Ghost descending upon the first apostles. Before the altar was set a large table on which there stood a gold chalice and a small golden platter. Near the table was a simple potbellied stove whose flue projected through a small window that looked out on the Square of St Peter.

When the voting took place, each cardinal would write the name of his candidate upon a ballot paper, lay it first on the golden platter, and then put it into the chalice, to signify that he had completed a sacred act. After the votes were counted, they would be burned in the stove, and smoke would issue through the flue into the Square of St Peter. To elect a Pope, there must be a majority of two-thirds.

If the majority were not conclusive, the ballot papers would be burned with wet straw, and the smoke would issue dark and cloudy. Only when the ballot was successful would the papers be burned without straw, so that a white smoke might inform the waiting crowds that they had a new Pope. It was an archaic and cumbersome ceremony for the age of radio and television, but it served to underline the drama of the moment and the continuity of two thousand years of papal history.

When all the cardinals were seated, the master of ceremonies made the circuit of the thrones, handing to each voter a single ballot paper. Then he left the chapel, and the door was locked, leaving only the princes of the Church to elect the successor to Peter.

It was the moment for which Leone and Rinaldi had waited. Leone rose in his place, tossed his white mane, and addressed the conclave:

'My brothers, I stand to claim a right under the Apostolic Constitution. I proclaim to you my belief that there is among us a man already chosen by God to sit in the Chair of Peter. Like the first of the apostles, he has suffered prison and stripes for the faith, and the hand of God has led him out of bondage to join us in this conclave. I announce him as my candidate, and dedicate to him my vote and my obedience . . . Kiril Cardinal Lakota.'

There was a moment of dead silence, broken by a stifled gasp from Lakota. Then Rahamani the Syrian rose in his place and pronounced firmly:

'I too proclaim him.'

'I too,' said Carlin the American.

'And I,' said Valerio Rinaldi.

Then in twos and threes, old men heaved themselves to their feet with a like proclamation until all but nine were standing under the canopies, while Kiril Cardinal Lakota sat, blank-faced and rigid, on his throne.

Then Rinaldi stepped forward and challenged the

electors. 'Does any here dispute that this is a valid election, and that a majority of more than two-thirds has elected our brother Kiril?'

No-one answered the challenge.

'Please be seated,' said Valerio Rinaldi.

As each cardinal sat down, he pulled the cord attached to his canopy so that it collapsed above his head, and the only canopy left open was that above the chair of Kiril Cardinal Lakota.

The Camerlengo rang a small hand bell and walked across to unlock the chapel door. Immediately there entered the secretary of the conclave, the master of ceremonies, and the sacristan of the Vatican. These three prelates, with Leone and Rinaldi, moved ceremoniously to the throne of the Ukrainian. In a loud voice Leone challenged him:

'*Acceptasne electionem?* Do you accept election?'

All eyes were turned on the tall, lean stranger with his scarred face and his dark beard and his distant, haunted eyes. Seconds ticked away slowly, and then in a dead flat voice, they heard him answer:

'*Accepto . . . Miserere mei Deus!* I accept. God have mercy on me!'

EXTRACT FROM THE SECRET MEMORIALS OF KIRIL I PONT. MAX.

No ruler can escape the verdict of history; but a ruler who keeps a diary makes himself liable to a rough handling by the judged. . . . I should hate to be like old Pius II, who had his memoirs attributed to his secretary, had them expurgated by his kinsmen and then, five hundred years later, had all his indiscretions restored by a pair of American blue-stockings. Yet I sympathise with his dilemma, which must be the dilemma of every man who sits in the Chair of Peter. A Pope can never talk freely unless he talks to God or to himself — and a Pontiff who talks to himself is apt to become eccentric, as the histories of some of my predecessors have shown.

It is my infirmity to be afraid of solitude and isolation. So I shall need some safety valves — the diary for one, which is a compromise between lying to oneself on paper and telling posterity the facts that have to be concealed from one's own generation. There is a rub, of course. What does one do with a papal diary? Leave it to the Vatican library? Order it buried with oneself in the triple coffin? Or auction it beforehand for the propagation of the faith? Better, perhaps, not to begin at all; but how else guarantee a vestige of privacy, humour, perhaps even sanity in this noble prison house to which I am condemned?

Twenty-four hours ago my election would have seemed a fantasy. Even now I cannot understand why I accepted it. I could have refused. I did not. Why? . . .

Consider what I am: Kiril I, Bishop of Rome, Vicar of Jesus Christ, Successor of the Prince of the Apostles, Supreme Pontiff of the Universal Church, Patriarch of the West, Primate of Italy, Archbishop and Metropolitan of the Roman Province, Sovereign of the Vatican City State . . . Gloriously reigning, of course . . . !

But this is only the beginning of it. The Pontifical Annual will print a list two pages long of what I have reserved by way of abbacies and prefectures, and what I shall 'protect' by way of orders, congregations, confraternities and holy sisterhoods. The rest of its two thousand pages will be a veritable Doomsday Book of my ministers and subjects, my instruments of government, education and correction.

I must be, by the very nature of my office, multilingual, though the Holy Ghost has been less generous in the gift of tongues to me than he was to the first man who stood in my shoes. My mother tongue is Russian; my official language is the Latin of the schoolmen, a kind of Mandarin which is supposed to preserve magically the subtlest definition of truth like a bee in amber. I must speak Italian to my associates and converse with all in that high-flown 'we' which hints at a secret converse between God and myself, even in such mundane matters as the coffee 'we' shall drink for breakfast and the brand of petrol 'we' shall use for Vatican City automobiles.

Still, this is the traditional mode and I must not resent it too much. Old Valerio Rinaldi gave me fair warning when an hour after this morning's election he offered me both his retirement and his loyalty. 'Don't try to change the Romans, Holiness. Don't try to fight them or convert them. They've been managing Popes for the last nineteen hundred years and they'll break your neck before you bend theirs. But walk softly, speak gently, keep your own counsel, and in the end you will twist them like grass round your fingers.'

It is too early, Heaven knows, to see what success Rome and I shall have with one another, but Rome is no longer the world, and I am not too much concerned — just so I can borrow experience from those who have pledged me their oaths as Cardinal Princes of the Church. There are some in whom I have great confidence. There are others . . . But I must not judge too swiftly. They cannot all be like Rinaldi, who is a wise and gentle man with a sense of humour and a knowledge of his own limitations. Meantime, I must try to smile and keep a good temper while I find my way round this Vatican maze. . . . And I must commit my thoughts to a diary before I expose them to curia or consistory.

I have an advantage, of course, in that no-one quite knows which way I shall jump — I don't even know myself. I am the first Slav ever to sit on the Chair of Peter, the first non-Italian for four-and-a-half centuries. The curia will be wary of me. They may have been inspired to elect me but already they must be wondering what kind of Tartar they have caught. Already they will be asking themselves how I shall reshuffle their appointments and spheres of influence. How can they know how much I am afraid and doubtful of myself? I hope some of them will remember to pray for me.

The Papacy is the most paradoxical office in the world; the most absolute and yet the most limited; the richest in revenues but the poorest in personal return. It was founded by a Nazarene carpenter who owned no place to rest His head, yet it is surrounded by more pomp and panoply than is seemly in this hungry world. It owns no frontiers, yet is subject always to national intrigue and partisan pressure. The man who accepts it claims divine guarantee against error, yet is less assured of salvation than the meanest of his subjects. The keys of the kingdom dangle at his belt, yet he can find himself locked out forever from the peace of election and the communion of saints. If he says he is not tempted by autocracy and ambition, he is a liar. If he does not walk sometimes in terror, and pray often in darkness, then he is a fool.

I know — or at least I am beginning to know. I was elected this morning, and tonight I am alone on the Mountain of Desolation. He whose vicar I am, hides His face from me. Those whose shepherd I must be do not know me. The world is spread beneath me like a campaign map — and I see balefires on every frontier. There are blind eyes upturned, and a babel of voices invoking an unknown . . .

O God, give me light to see, and strength to know, and courage to endure the servitude of the servants of God . . . !

My valet has just been in to prepare my sleeping quarters. He is a melancholy fellow who looks very like a guard in Siberia who used to curse me at night for a Ukrainian dog and each morning for an adulterous priest. This one, however, asks humbly if my Holiness has need of anything. Then he kneels and begs my blessing on himself and his family. Embarrassed, he ventures to suggest that, if I am not too tired, I may deign to show myself again to the people who still wait in St Peter's Square.

They acclaimed me this morning when I was led out to give my first blessing to the city and to the world. Yet, so long as my light burns, it seems there will always be some waiting for God knows what sign of power of benignity from the papal bedroom. How can I tell them that they must never expect too much from a middle-aged fellow in striped cotton pyjamas? But tonight is different. There is a whole concourse of Romans and of tourists in the Piazza, and it would be a courtesy — excuse me, Holiness, a great condescension! — to appear with one small blessing . . .

I condescend, and I am exalted once again on wave after wave of cheering and horn-blowing. I am their Pope, their Father, and they urge me to live a long time. I bless them and hold out my arms to them, and they clamour again, and I am caught in a strange heart-stopping moment when it seems that my arms encompass the world, and that it is much too heavy for me to hold. Then my valet — or is it my jailer? — draws me back, closes the window and draws the drapes, so that, officially at least, His Holiness Kiril I is in bed and asleep.

The valet's name is Celasio, which is also the name of a Pope. He is a good fellow, and I am glad of a minute of his company. We talk a few moments and then he asks me, blushing and stammering, about my name. He is the first who has dared to raise the question except old Rinaldi, who, when I announced that I desired to keep my baptismal name, nodded and smiled ironically and said, 'A noble style, Holiness — provocative, too. But for God's sake don't let them turn it into Italian.'

I took his advice, and I explained to the cardinals as I now explain to my valet that I kept the name because it belonged to the Apostle of the Slavs, who was said to have invented the modern Cyrillic alphabet and who was a stubborn defender of the right of people to keep the faith in their own idiom. I explained to them also that I should prefer to have my name used in its Slavic form, for a testimony to the universality of the Church. Not all of them approved since they are quick to see how a man's first act sets the pattern of his later ones.

No-one objected, however, except Leone, he who runs the Holy Office and has the reputation of a modern St Jerome, whether for his love of tradition, a spartan life, or a notoriously crusty temper I have yet to find out. Leone asked pointedly whether a Slavic name might not look out of place in the pure Latin of Papal Encyclicals. Although he is the one who first proclaimed me in the conclave, I had to tell him gently that I was more interested in having my encyclicals read by the people than in coddling the Latinists, and that since Russian had become a canonical language for the Marxist world, it would not hurt us to have the tip of one shoe in the other camp.

He took the reproof well, but I do not think he will easily forget it. Men who serve God professionally are apt to regard Him as a private preserve. Some of them would like to make His Vicar a private preserve as well. I do not say that Leone is one of these, but I have to be careful. I shall have to work differently from any of my predecessors, and I cannot submit myself to the dictate of any man, however high he stands, or however good he may be.

None of this, of course, is for my valet, who will take home only a simple tale of missionary saints and make himself a great man on the strength of a Pontiff's confidence. *Osservatore Romano* will tell exactly the same tale tomorrow, but for them it will be 'a symbol of the paternal care of His Holiness for those who cleave, albeit in good faith, to schismatic communions . . .' I must, as soon as I can, do something about the *Osservatore*. . . . If my voice is to be heard in the world it must be heard in its authentic tones.

Already I know there are questions about my beard. I have heard murmurs of a 'too Byzantine look'. The Latins are more sensitive about such customs than we are; so perhaps it might have been a courtesy to explain that my jaw was broken under questioning and that without a beard I am somewhat disfigured . . . It is so small a matter, and yet schisms have begun over smaller ones.

I wonder what Kamenev said when he heard the news of my election. I wonder whether he had humour enough to send me a greeting.

I am tired — tired to my bones and afraid. My charge is so simple: to keep the faith pure and bring the scattered sheep safely into the fold. Yet into what strange country it may lead me I can only guess . . . Lead us not into temptation, O Lord, but deliver us from evil. Amen.

Wire

—————

TIM WINTON

It's midnight in a free country a week before Christmas
with the war receding like the tide, and the celebrations
already forgotten. A dray-load of men trundles down
the limestone road. There's been two-up and boxes of
home brew tonight, and plenty of talk, too much of it.
A bottle of whisky does the rounds on the decline
toward the solitary light by the sea. Two horses shiver
and shake their steamy manes and the moon hovers in
the treetops. Somewhere a mopoke calls with some
hesitation. Pipes flare and glow, and one pecks on the
wagon's tray. Two figures do not smoke. They are rigid
and wide-eyed, the only sober passengers aboard. The
ocean growls down there. A light down there. A shack
down there.

A man appears with a lantern and the dray rolls to a stop outside the tin shack.

'Gentlemen.'

'Ah, Hanford.'

The man called Hanford holds the lantern high and sees the farmers and lumpers on the dray. He sees the boys with them, sees their eyes, their naked limbs, their hands over their balls. In the lamplight they are the colour of Keen's curry powder. He tries to think quickly.

'What's this, then, Mister Buckridge?'

'Oh, just some unfinished business.'

Hanford looks at the Tanaka boys, smells the booze, sees the shotgun broken across a farmer's lap.

'The war's over, Mister Buckridge.'

'It'll be over tonight, that's a fact.'

'I know about your boy.'

'Well, then you know.'

'He was a soldier. They're kids.'

'An eye for an eye, Hanford.'

'They've got nothing to do with it, and you know it. Why don't you leave 'em here with me.'

Buckridge laughs. Already Hanford sees there'll be no stopping this. This is something he could not have imagined in his direst sleep. He has fought fires with these men, kicked a football with them, ruffled their children's hair. Outside the glow of the lamp there is only darkness, and in it the moon. Inside the shack his own son sleeps.

'Go home, you blokes.'

They look to the big man Buckridge. They're all too old or crafty to have fought, but now their blood is up.

'Your boat, Hanford, that's all.'

Hanford considers all the things still to be said, but the boat is all he has; it blocks out every other thought. It's his living.

He swallows. 'Where?'

'The island. We won't need you.'

'I can't let you have it.'

'Oh?'

That's all Buckridge has to say. Hanford sees it all before him, the shack a smoking ruin.

'I'll have to take you myself. You're all bloody farmers, for Chrissake.'

'Don't let's start making social comparisons, Jock. It sounds like envy. You sounds like a fuckin bolshie.'

'I said I'd take you, you bastards.'

Hanford looks at his boots, cracked as the droughted earth. The laces are undone and he's had no time for socks in his haste.

'Give me a second.'

He goes back inside, holds the lamp near the boy's face a moment, then puts it on the deal table and dresses properly. For a moment he looks at the .22 standing against the far wall and considers the possibil- ities, but the sound of the boy's breathing cautions him. The boat and the boy, that's all of it. Jesus Christ, that's the choice.

Outside, he douses the lantern and shoots the bolt of the door. A bird leaves its roost on the roof.

'Mister Hanfor? Please, Mister Hanfor—'

He hears the blows as he pulls his coat on in the dark.

Someone hands him a bottle and he takes a long draft which tunnels coldly into him and ignites far down inside. Two men emerge from his lean-to shed with a big, glinting coil of barbed wire, new this week. He sets his teeth and climbs up on the dray. He does not look back at the naked boys. He sets his fists like blocks.

The horses move off at a walk through the salty wet air. The dray shudders down the ruts, the wheels turn, the bottle passes around. A roo lumbers back off the track and moves through the bush with the sound of a beating.

The boy is alone in the shack. The eye of the moon follows Hanford across the tops of the tuarts and peppermints. He wants it to be morning and a clear, grey dawn with a cold trough of water to wash in, kitchen smoke in his face, the sound of the boy's feet on the lino.

'What about their father?' he asks Buckridge. 'They're letting them out of the camps now.'

'Mister Hanfor!'

'Shut up, all of you!'

'Sit back, Tojo.'

'For Chrissake.'

'Just shut up.'

The dray stops where the track peters out against the dunes. They get down and walk in white sand. Hanford smells the minty scrub. In the cove the moon makes a puffy scar on the sea. An upturned dory lies high on the beach. Beneath it are oars, anchor chain, rowlocks.

One of the boys falls to his knees and begins to weep. His flesh shines.

'Get it organised, Hanford.'

Buckridge's voice pitches higher than normal. Hanford hears the son lost in Borneo, hears it in the man's throat. He hears the fresh stories in that voice: Changi, the railway, the jungle, the horror that still has not settled properly on the district. Hanford heard the story of how they found young Billy Buckridge's body, of his mates on their knees puking at the sight.

Two men help Hanford turn the boat and haul it down to the water. Small waves knock against the bow. The Tanaka boys are shoved in and a man climbs in with a shotgun while Buckridge himself helps Hanford push the boat out of the shallows, and as Hanford takes the oars the others stand on the beach looking furtive all of a sudden, spooked by the scuttling crabs, perhaps sobering up. They become mere shapes, then he's around the headland and they disappear. At his feet the boys shiver in the bottom of the boat, the steam of their piss rising.

The channel deepens and broadens, and as they clear the headland the swell comes thick and languorous. Over his shoulder, the shadow of the island. He catches the look on Buckridge's face in the moonlight. He's back to being a farmer now, worried by the water, and for a moment Hanford considers a way to unseat the bastard. But then he thinks of the shotgun behind him, the spraying hole his chest would be before him.

'You'll be wantin work this new year,' Buckridge says as they close on the island. 'Everyone's gearin up now that the fellas are back.'

'I wouldn't say no.'

'Well, that's settled then.' Buckridge lights his pipe and the light flaring under his chin renders him a childhood nightmare.

Yeah, that's it, then, Hanford thinks, pulling hard into calm water in the lee; that's it for bloody sure. That's it.

He moves them around the limestone bluff where a thousand terns stir.

'Right, let us off here.'

'There's no landing spot here.'

'Let us off now.'

Hanford smells shit. He punts in to the base of the bluff and feels the keel scrape.

'Go. Go now or we'll hole the boat.'

Buckridge leaps out and the boat rises gaily free of his weight. 'Come on, boys.'

The Tanaka boys hug each other in the bottom of the boat. Hanford feels a twinge of disgust. The coil of barbed wire flies over his head. He hadn't even seen it in the boat. God Almighty.

'You can hug all you like, lads,' says the man with the weapon. 'Now get out of the fuckin boat.'

The twin barrels come over Hanford's shoulder by his right ear. Then suddenly they tilt skyward and flash. The sound knocks Hanford sideways and the boys scuttle out as pellets hit the water, bounce slackly on the limestone.

The man clambers over him and Buckridge's mouth is moving, but all Hanford hears is a ghostly ringing. He shoves off blindly and watches them climb. In deep water the anchor rope burns through his hands. He sits there with his ears ringing, mercifully unable to hear what it sounds like for two boys to be bound together with barbed wire, thinking that, as his life goes: being married, deserted, fleeced and ground down, this probably constitutes a lucky break. It takes this. This to feed his kid. This.

The sky fills with fleeing birds. They hear it. Ten thousand birds hear it. Three hundred yards of wire. It will take more than a few minutes. The flickering cloud of birds boils in the moonlight, and Hanford prays that the sea would swallow him up, that his son had not been born, that they would hurry up and get it over with.

At dawn he lights the stove. The sharp eucalypt tang of smoke wakes the boy.

'I had a dream the Devil came.'

'Just a dream, son.'

Hanford goes outside for wood. Piles of dung stand in the road. Just a dream, he thinks, fetching the shovel.

Enigma of Exile:
a Passage, a Death

———•———

SATENDRA NANDAN

There is, of course, no such thing as a bloodless coup. All coups are like heart attacks — something inside silently dies while the heart haemorrhages. And so it was for my country, Fiji, after the two coups of 1987, when the Colonel ruthlessly robbed Fiji of its very heart.

But that time and place were an age and an ocean away as I left my office in Canberra late one Friday afternoon almost three years later. I usually did this to catch the early evening news and the 'PM' program. The headlines that day announced 'Fiji's Former Prime Minister Dies.' For a moment I hoped against hope that it wasn't Doctor Timoci Bavadra, for in my mind he had never become 'former'. Doc, as he was affectionately known, was for me and for thousands of others the elected and legitimate Prime Minister of the people of Fiji.

My hopes were soon crushed and the news of his passing was a shock, a sorrow, as death always is no matter how expected, how seemingly natural. My last image of Doc was on the night after a television recording of 'Hypothetical' in Canberra during his visit to Australia earlier that year. After the long hours of recording, a handful of us wanted to take Doc home for a drink. He declined, saying he felt tired and wanted to rest. It was already past midnight. Wishing us goodnight and God bless, he walked away from us, followed a couple of paces behind by his young son. As we watched from the steps, he disappeared into the darkness of a winter's night in Canberra.

Thinking of Doc took my thoughts back to that other time and place, to Fiji and the events that lead to the two coups.

———•———

The lives and livelihood of Fijians have always been closely linked to the sea and somehow they have long withstood the vagaries of natural disasters, whether hurricanes or floods. When the hurricanes pass and the winds that can destroy whole villages have gone their troublesome way, the people emerge from the remnants of their houses and begin anew. Someone always produces a bowl of grog from somewhere and, fortified, they start the process of digging post holes for a new home on perhaps another spot. My father did that often — his homes were never strongly built. But I do not know if my brothers and sisters and their children will have the courage, endurance and the lust for life to continue building on a graveyard.

Today, more than fifty members of my extended

family are out of Fiji. Most of them are professional people: doctors, lawyers, engineers, librarians, academics, teachers and small business men and women. Fiji was our home — most of us had known no other place, and no-one from my family had ever migrated to another country. Now we are dispossessed, dislocated, disenfranchised.

I had been a member of parliament for five years, fought and won two elections and became Minister for Health and Social Welfare in Prime Minister Timoci Bavadra's first multiracial cabinet.

I have many memories of Doc, but I especially remember his magnificent speech as the Leader of the Coalition given at the Girmit Centre at Lautoka, significantly created to commemorate the arrival of the first indentured Indians to Fiji in 1879.

When the election victory was announced in April 1987, Doc had attained the unimaginable against overwhelming odds: his human and humane policy of multiracialism and a truly democratic government had won. We felt it was a victory for Fiji's history, its heritage and future. For the first time in our nation's life, he created a genuine multiracial cabinet and government.

Two days after our amazing electoral victory Prime Minister Bavadra invited me to his office and offered me the Health Ministry, and told me jovially that he was giving me the shit ministry! I accepted, but I remembered the words of my brother, who was a medical practitioner, warning me of the cholesterol of indecisions and maladministration that flowed in the arteries of the Health Department. But I must say I found the prospect of being Minister for Health very attractive. I felt this was an area where I could improve the lot of the ordinary people of Fiji.

In only thirty-three days of power as the Prime Minister of Fiji, Doc changed Fiji's destiny. And so, when it happened, the first coup came as a great betrayal. It was ironic that a country which had not known a single political prisoner suddenly had a whole government abducted and imprisoned. I do not think he and many others ever recovered from the enormity of that crime.

It was the morning of 14 May, barely a month after taking office, when I was doing a radio talkback show as the Health Minister at the Fiji Broadcasting Commission. It was a good opportunity to explain the new government's policies. In only one month, by sheer hard work, we had done more to restore the faith of the people in the government than the whole of the previous Alliance's seventeen years in office.

After the interview I went straight to parliament. At the end of the prayer we all said 'Amen' and sat down. It was unfortunate that a member of the Opposition was scheduled to deliver a rather boring maiden speech and, losing interest in what was being said, I moved to leave my seat as a mark of my disinterest. As I turned to leave I was handed a note from the Minister of Finance, asking if I would draft a speech for one of our colleagues. I had just written the first sentence when a foolish statement by the Alliance member made me interject: 'Address the Chair, you larrikin!' These were the last legitimate words of the Fiji Parliament as we had known it.

Suddenly there was a commotion in the chamber and, as I raised my eyes, I saw the Colonel, dressed neatly in civilian clothes, closely followed by ten masked gunmen wearing gas masks and carrying guns. Those guns were cocked and ready to be used.

Still in a state of shock we were herded out of parliament, one by one behind Dr Bavadra and put into two army trucks. I thought it curious that Militoni, the former Alliance Minister who was now Speaker of the House, was not among us. The trucks drove off, and with no possibility of escape we sat in silence.

We were taken to the Queen Elizabeth Barracks. As we drove through the iron gates one of the new Labour politicians naively whispered to me not to be alarmed as he thought it was just a rehearsal, in case of some problems in parliament. Some rehearsal! How wrong he was.

For the next five nights, and in the full glare of a global spotlight, we were to glimpse the heart of darkness.

———

Initially the soldiers tried to put us into several small stinking cells which we refused to enter. It was only Doc's authoritative presence which stood as a shield between us and our captors. Doc prevailed and we remained in the front room. Just as our collective drama was unfolding, other personal family dramas were being played out in our homes, not the least my own.

My wife, Jyoti, and one of my daughters were listening to the radio when the unbelievable became reality. An hour later they were told I had been shot because of my earlier clash with the Alliance member in Parliament. I still feel an immense anger at the anguish and grief this caused Jyoti.

Early that afternoon we were taken to the officers' mess in small groups. By now a few curious people who knew what was happening had gathered at the entrance to the Royal Barracks, even though the gates were closed and patrolled by soldiers with guns. We waved to several familiar faces, and one, a reporter from the *Fiji Times*, recognised me and eventually contacted my wife to tell her I was alive and well.

We were in fact allowed to move around inside the officers mess, and some of my colleagues played pool while others chose to view the trophies and memorabilia of soldiers who had distinguished themselves in the service of the Empire. We were allowed to call our families that evening, but for some reason we were not fed, and we were left in no doubt by our captors that they meant business — this was for real. Eventually, in the quiet and dark of night, we were reloaded into military jeeps and taken to the Prime Minister's residence.

During our first three nights in detention — the first day in the small military cell, later at the Prime Minister's residence — Doc held us together by his inner strength, his calm, courageous voice, and his immense tenderness. He had a great deal of it — how else can one explain a Director of Family Planning with eleven happy children.

I managed to find a few scraps of paper during our detention at Doc's house, and set about keeping notes of my thoughts and events as they unfolded. I was forced to write my diary in secret, sometimes in the toilet, until eventually the guards realised what I was doing and most of my pages were confiscated. Only a few, which I had managed to secrete in one of my socks, were saved.

We prayed a lot before every meagre meal. I've never seen twenty-eight more devout members of parliament. I must confess I often said the longest prayer and Doc would ask before every meal, 'Where's Rev Dr Nadan?' And then the PM's house would reverberate with his spontaneous laughter. During our imprisonment I was heard to say a number of times that there would be light at the end of the tunnel. Finally, one morning Doc whispered to me, 'Saten, I think your tunnel is getting longer every day.' His laughter and that of his companions surprised and bewildered the guards.

By Friday of that week we were allowed to change our clothes and our wives were permitted to visit in the presence of the soldiers. They came, one by one, fearful, tearful and tragic. The next day wore on full of mounting tension: hundreds had gathered outside the gate of Doc's residence, despite the barbed wire rolled out to keep them away. Dr Bavadra was allowed to stroll in his garden, causing the waiting crowd to applaud thunderously.

Soon the soldiers came in asking for two members of parliament, Krishna Dutt and Kalou, but we refused to hand them over. Someone said that this was the beginning: we'd be shot two by two. Later the soldiers came back and asked for Tupeni Baba and Harish Sharma, then James Shanker Singh and me. Again we refused to surrender them, and the bewildered soldiers finally gave up. All of us would go, or none.

On that terrible Sunday when the powers that held the guns decided to segregate the MPs on racial lines, Doc was determined it wouldn't happen. The resistance began at six in the morning and continued for three hours. Suddenly armed soldiers burst in to drag us from Doc's *bure* to waiting landrovers parked about two hundred metres away. I lay on the dirt road where two young soldiers tried to lift me and failed. The Deputy PM was snatched from Doc's arms, and then a huge soldier came and threw me unceremoniously into the back seat of the landrover with a bruising thud.

When we were released a week later, Doc quizzed me as we went to his simple home:

'Do you know who threw you into the landrover?'

I shook my head. All soldiers at the time looked the same to me.

'You know it was your driver from the Health Ministry!'

Then he gave his famous, free laugh and I forgot my painful back.

But at that time, as we were being so roughly man-handled, I thought we'd never see Doc or his splendid wife, Adi Kuini, again. We were separated from our Fijian colleagues and our Prime Minister and taken to more spacious quarters at Borron House. This was a cunning move by our captors, as together we were strong and resolute, but separated we were weakened, at least psychologically.

The Speaker of the House, Mr Militoni Leweniqila, descended from an upstairs room, not unlike Moses. But unlike Moses, he carried two bottles of whisky, and as he came towards us he boomed, 'Order! Order!'

Militoni amused us for the next two hours with colourful stories and reverberating laughter. Eventually I proposed that we, the Indian MPs, should go on a hunger strike to protest against our forced segregation. But this Gandhian gesture didn't impress Militoni, and when he heard this suggestion he went upstairs for lunch, saying he would be back in the evening. His departure plunged us into gloom.

Hungry and demoralised, most of us found places to sleep during the midday heat. Despite the heat, and perhaps more to escape the relentless gaze of the soldiers, several of the older MPs covered themselves with blankets. About an hour later we noticed one young member's blanket moving up and down somewhere around where his mouth should be. Thinking he was having a fit, one of my colleagues flung the blanket off the man on the sofa, only to find a young MP, supposedly on a hunger strike, munching a juicy apple. Our laughter relieved the tension and bewildered our sullen guards.

Sadly though, our hunger strike did not last beyond one meal and I was told by one of my colleagues not to suggest such Gandhian ideas again.

Later that afternoon we could see people gathering on a hill nearby. They obviously knew we were being held in Borron House, particularly as the soldiers were guarding it so closely. From time to time we managed to wave from the windows, and once they saw us they clapped and cheered. This brought the guards rushing in to close the curtains.

It is perhaps not insignificant that as the coup leaders were deciding what to do with the Prime Minister and his government during the following days, one suggestion was to send them to Makogai — an island on which Fiji's lepers were quarantined. The island, sadly, may yet become a symbol of the archipelago.

Finally, on the following Tuesday, we began to get an inkling that something was about to happen. Our captors were showing signs of unease, whispering and moving about inside and outside. At about ten that evening we were suddenly allowed to leave, and carrying our pathetic little bundles of belongings, we left Borron House and returned to our loved ones.

—————

After the first coup we still had hope that it was possible to bring the derailed constitutional train back on the tracks, and slowly we'd add compartments to it. We worked quietly but effectively.

Dr Bavadra asked me to prepare a paper on the

situation, and eventually a deal was struck at Deuba — in my constituency. We believed our team had done well in the circumstances. Then, two days later, as I was enjoying my siesta after a heavy and happy lunch, the Colonel (by then a General) struck again. Once again we were caught napping. The second coup was, in my opinion, the more fatal.

And so, barely six months later, I was forced to accept that there was no longer a place for me in Fiji. I arrived at Nandi Airport on Thursday 3 December, 1987, around 10.10 a.m., to catch an Air Pacific flight to Sydney. My recollections are so precise because I was about to make the longest journey of my life. I was leaving my country, Fiji.

Two days before, I had driven to the gates of Queen Elizabeth Barracks, the headquarters and home of the Royal Fiji Military Forces — still 'Royal' after two treasonable coups. It was here that we had been confined after our abduction during the first coup and now I made my second visit to ask permission to leave Fiji. I parked my car outside and walked up to the gate.

I introduced myself to a rather gruff soldier who seemed to recognise my name, and immediately two more guards came out and opened the gates. I explained my reasons for coming and told them I needed to see their commander.

I think they were so bewildered by my sudden appearance that one of them immediately rushed inside and rang someone. While I waited I looked over the decrepit building where we were interned for three brutal hours, committing its measurements to memory as I stared at the grim concrete floor on which we had sat. Some of my colleagues had wept.

Eventually the soldier came out and said, 'Sir, the officer will see you. Please come with me.'

I was equally polite, said thank you, and together we marched towards the officers mess. By now several soldiers were whispering among themselves and casting furtive glances at me. A lawyer friend, whom I had asked to accompany me to the barracks, had declined, warning, 'I'm not a suicidal samurai, pal. Don't go in there!' But I had to — more from compulsion than courage.

People like me had to get permission to travel outside Fiji and several of my colleagues who had tried earlier were harassed at the airport and refused permission to leave. Our names apparently were on a computer list, and although I'd applied a month earlier, there was no reply from the Suva Police. Two days before departure my wife, Jyoti, was getting tense. She didn't want to leave without me so, without telling her, I had driven to the barracks to get the necessary permission.

Set on a gentle slope between the prison house and the officers mess was another building. I hadn't noticed it on the day of the coup. Today there it was, neat and tidy, full of soldiers and officers in uniform. I was taken into a room and given a chair. In a couple of minutes an officer came in looking well fed and important. Everyone saluted as I sat. He extended his hand to me warmly and with a handsome smile asked, 'What can I do for you, sir?'

I explained. Immediately he rang somewhere and there was an agitated conversation lasting about fifteen minutes. Then he put the phone down, smiled at me, and said, 'All is okay, sir. You can leave on Thursday.'

'What about a letter?' I asked anxiously.

'There is no need,' he replied.

My name had been struck off the dreaded computer list. I was escorted out with great courtesy and the gates closed behind me. I drove straight home humming a Hindi film song.

In the evening I told everyone what I had done. Jyoti was still uncertain if I'd be allowed to leave as I didn't have the letter. You couldn't trust the words of these soldiers — after all, they had taken an oath of allegiance to the Queen and the elected Government of Fiji, and then had staged two coups.

The hour at the airport prior to our departure was fraught with anxiety and event. My wife and two daughters waited nervously in the departure lounge when I was asked to step aside after showing my passport to a pugnacious looking official. They had to check with military headquarters to find out if I was allowed to leave Fiji.

After a while it was obvious that the official had deliberately forgotten me. While I waited I went into Motibhai's duty free shop and bought a bottle of Royal Salute for a friend in Canberra. I eventually passed on that bottle of Royal Salute, the only one I've bought in my life. Rather regrettably, my friend didn't invite me to share it, so I still don't know how Royal Salute tastes. Ironically, the Commander of the Royal Military Forces has declared Fiji a republic, presumably enjoying all the 'royal salutes' himself.

Finally, the departure of Air Pacific was announced and I joined the queue of eager passengers. As we sat on the tarmac waiting for take off, I wondered if someone would come and remove me from the plane, as had happened to my political colleagues. Finally, the Air Pacific flight was airborne. People used to call it 'air pathetic' for its poor service, and yet this morning — for me and many others — this much-maligned airline was our flight to freedom.

The plane circled over my village, barely three kilometres from the airport. Below I could see the stony patch of land where I used to graze cattle. Earlier that morning I had seen my mother's tears as I left my brother's home. She stood framed in the doorway, wiping her eyes with her white, widow's 'orhini'. I hadn't even said good-bye to my brothers or sisters, other than the one with whom I'd spent the night. He'd dropped us at the airport and gone to his work at Vuda Point where the first Fijians were supposed to have landed. There are many myths in paradise.

As the plane circled I felt the sense of sadness one feels when leaving a cremation ground as the embers are dying and ashes take over. I had made so many journeys from Nandi airport in the past — all of them happy. Then I looked at my wife and children and the vast ocean below. My mood changed and I ordered a bottle of champagne. But still, I couldn't help thinking of some lines from T S Eliot's *To the Indians Who Died in Africa*:

> A man's destination is not his destiny,
> Every country is home to one man
> And exile to another. Where a man dies bravely
> At one with his destiny, that soil is his.

Contributors

Thea Astley, one of Australia's most acclaimed and prolific writers, was born in 1925 in Brisbane, and studied at the University of Queensland. She has published twelve novels since 1958, and is a triple winner of the Miles Franklin Award for *The Well Dressed Explorer* in 1962, *The Slow Natives* in 1965 and for *The Acolyte* in 1972. She also won The Age Book of the Year Award for *A Kindness Cup*, and the Townsville Literary Foundation Award in 1979 for her collection of short stories, *Hunting the Wild Pineapple*. She won the Australian Literature Society Gold Medal in 1987 for her novel *Beachmasters*, and the Steele Rudd Award and the FAW ANA Literature Award in 1988 for *It's Raining in Mango*. In 1990 Thea Astley won the New South Wales State Literary Award for fiction with *Reaching Tin River*. Her latest book, *Vanishing Points*, was published in 1992.

Thea Astley writes full time and lives in the hills on the New South Wales south coast.

Manning Clark was born in Sydney in 1915 and educated at Melbourne Grammar and the University of Melbourne. He later attended Balliol College, Oxford, and taught history at schools in England and Australia in the early 1940s. He became senior lecturer at the University of Melbourne and Professor of History at the Australian National University, Canberra, where, in 1972 he became the first Professor of Australian History. He wrote his major life's work, *A History of Australia*, in six volumes, between 1962 and 1987, thereafter radically changing the way Australians think of themselves. He was made a Companion of the Order of Australia in 1975, and named Australian of the Year in 1980. Professor Manning Clark died in May 1991.

Bryce Courtenay, advertising executive, columnist and author, was born in South Africa in 1933 and became an Australian citizen 34 years ago. He is a regular speaker with Harry M. Miller Speakers Bureau. His first book, *The Power of One*, became an international bestseller and film, has been translated into 11 languages and has sold close to one million copies. His second novel, *Tandia*, has also become a bestseller. His latest book, *April Fools Day*, was published in April 1993.

Sara Dowse was born in Chicago, USA, and lived in New York and Los Angeles before migrating to Australia in 1958. She has worked as a journalist, editor, academic, and public servant, and her work has appeared in a range of publications. Her first novel, *West Block* (1983), is based on her experiences as head of the federal government's Office of Women's Affairs in the 1970s. Two novels — *Silver City* and *Schemetime* — were published later, as was her contribution to *Canberra Tales*, a collection of stories compiled by Seven Writers and published for the bicentenary in 1988. Her next work of fiction, *Safar: To Count*, is due to be published soon.

Suzanne Edgar was born and grew up in Adelaide, but moved to Canberra in 1963. Since 1976 she has worked part time as an editor on the *Australian Dictionary of Biography*. In 1984 she joined the group Seven Writers, with whom she published *Canberra Tales* (1988). Her book *Counting Backwards* (1991) was shortlisted for the 1992 Steele Rudd short story award and she is currently completing a novel. She and her husband have two daughters.

Libby Hathorn was born in Newcastle, New South Wales, and has written extensively for children as well as writing adult fiction and poetry. Several of her books have won awards in the Australian Children's Book of the Year Awards, including her young adult novel *Thunderwith* which has been translated into five languages and has won an award in the Netherlands (1992). Her adult fiction includes *Better Strangers* (1991). She is currently working on a children's opera based on her text *Grandma's Shoes*. Her latest novels for young adults are *Valley Under the Rock* and the forthcoming *Feral Kid* which is about homeless children in Sydney.

Dorothy Johnston is the author of three novels: *Tunnel Vision*, *Ruth*, and *Maralinga My Love*. Her short stories have been widely published, two of them appearing in the anthology, *Canberra Tales*, written by the Seven Writers Group, of which she is a member. She was the winner of the inaugural ACT Literary Award in 1991. She was born in Geelong, Victoria, in 1948, and has lived in Canberra since 1979. She has two children.

Nicholas Jose has travelled widely and lived and worked in England, Italy, Australia and China after completing tertiary studies at the Australian National University and Oxford University. From 1987 to 1990 he was Cultural Counsellor at the Australian Embassy, Peking. Since 1990 he has lived in Sydney and writes full-time. His publications include two collections of short stories, *The Possession of Amber* and *Feathers or Lead* and three novels, *Rowena's*

Field, *Paper Nautilus* and *Avenue of Eternal Peace* which was adapted for television. He is currently working on a novel, a television drama series about a Chinese family in Australia and a translation project.

Tom Keneally was born in 1935 and educated in Sydney. One of Australia's foremost novelists, his publications include *The Chant of Jimmy Blacksmith* (also a film), *Confederates* and *Gossip From the Forest* (both short-listed for the Booker Prize), as well as *Schindler's Ark* (which won the 1982 Booker Prize and has sold more copies than any other winner before or since). *The Playmaker*, published in 1947, formed the basis for an award-winning play, *Our Country's Good*. Tom Keneally is married with two daughters. His latest book is *Our Republic* reflecting his passionate satirical interest in Australian republicanism, and his forthcoming novel, *Jacko*, is set in Sydney, the Northern Territory and New York.

Satendra Nandan, born in Fiji, became the first Labour MP and Minister for Health, Social Welfare and Women's Affairs in the Coalition Government of 1987. After the second coup he came to Canberra in 1987 to take up a Fellowship at the Australian National University. He has published two volumes of poetry, *Faces in a Village* and *Voices in the River*, as well as his first novel *The Wounded Sea* in 1991. He is currently teaching in the Faculty of Communication at the University of Canberra. This piece is from his forthcoming memoir *Relics of a Rainbow* to be published in 1994.

Morris West is one of the world's greatest story-tellers: a novelist with a clear style and a willingness to tackle large subjects of common concern. His books (more than 20 and published in some 27 languages), have sold tens of millions of copies. Among his best known books, some of which became films, are *The Devil's Advocate*, *Shoes of the Fisherman*, *The Ambassador*, *The Tower of Babel* and *The Salamander*. Born in Melbourne in 1916, he has led a varied life as a teaching monk, a cipher expert, private secretary to Prime Minister William Morris Hughes, and as a producer of radio serials and dramas. He has lived in Austria, England, and Italy, and received many literary awards, including the James Tait Black Memorial Prize, the Royal Society of Literature Heinemann Award, the National Brotherhood Award, and the National Council of Christians and Jews award. He was invested as a Member of the Order of Australia in 1985.

Tim Winton is widely regarded as one of Australia's most exciting young writers. Born in 1960, he has won every major literary award in Australia, including the Australian/ Vogel Award with his first novel, *An Open Swimmer*, and the Miles Franklin Award for his second novel, *Shallows*. His most recent novel, *Cloudstreet*, has been both a literary and commercial success, and was a joint winner of both the NBC Banjo Award for fiction and the West Australian Fiction Award, as well as the Deo Gloria Award in the United Kingdom. In 1992 *Cloudstreet* won the Miles Franklin Award. Several of his novels have been translated into French, Dutch and Swedish. He has also published two collections of short stories and books for children. Tim lives in a fishing village in Western Australia with his wife and children and is currently at work on a new novel. The excerpt included in this volume is taken from a work in progress.